Gallery Books
Editor: Peter Fallon
THE WORD FOR YES

Tom Mac Intyre

THE WORD FOR YES

New and selected stories

Gallery Books

The Word for Yes
is first published
simultaneously in paperback
and in a clothbound edition
on 28 November 1991.

The Gallery Press
Loughcrew
Oldcastle
County Meath
Ireland

*All rights reserved. For permission
to reprint or broadcast these stories,
write to The Gallery Press.*

© Tom Mac Intyre 1970, 1982, 1991

ISBN 1 85235 069 5 (*paperback*)
    1 85235 070 9 (*clothbound*)

The Gallery Press receives financial assistance from An Chomhairle
Ealaíon / The Arts Council, Ireland.

Contents

from DANCE THE DANCE
    Stallions *page* 11
    The Great Sword 14
    Willy Wynne, Con Moto 20
    Gunning's Word 27
    An Aspect of the Rising 33

from THE HARPER'S TURN
    Boarding 37
    The Hurt Mind 40
    The Windy Tree 42
    Deer Crossing 45
    The Mankeeper 50
    The Harper's Turn 55
    Cliodhna's Wave 60
    The Hospital Barber 63
    Left of the Door 65

NEW STORIES
    Thalassa 67
    Ghost Children 69
    Pot Black 72
    Foggy Hair and Green Eyes 76
    Wing-Beat, Wing-Feather 82
    The Word for Yes 88
    Rise Up Lovely Sweeney 93

*for four women
and maybe a fifth*

Stallions

One afternoon the housekeeper pounced.
 —You're going to the creamery, the can pushed at me, two shillings worth of cream and hurry back.
 I went down the avenue and on to the road where tar oozed and gleamed after hours of sun.
 The town lay a good shout off, the creamery half a mile beyond. I set out, past Jack Traynor's who had been a schoolmaster, was now old, and came abroad only to walk in the downpour; past Miss Farnan's who snatched kindling from behind hedges and had seen the Blessed Virgin; past Tom Millar's who housed a motor-bike and greyhounds but was Protestant. I stopped at Carroll's archway, that day a funnel of shadows. My eyes pricked. Among the shadows, sloping round the curve which hid the gap of the other end, was Albert McElwaine.
 There was something up in Carroll's yard.
 McElwaine was about my age, his curiosity mine. The cut of him lured me, the lie of his back, the drag of his hand as he took the bend — blurring himself to the wall. I followed, hastening through, round the blind curve and into the yard, a square which held the light like a bowl.
 Ten or twenty men were standing about, talking in groups, smoking, testing the ground with ashplants or nubbly black-thorns. A line of carts to one side, cherry and blue, shafts down, backsides up, harness slack in their bellies, had gone to sleep. There was a green whiff of droppings, and the stomping and tossing of horses fidgety in the dark stables. Nothing was happening. McElwaine, by himself in a far corner, hadn't seen me yet.
 From behind the row of carts, someone brought out a black

mare, shivery patches of sweat slick on her rump. In the middle of the yard they stopped, waiting, the middle their own. The space had grown while they moved into it. The mare jibbed and wheeled.

As if a thousand locks had snapped, a door to the left flew open. A stallion ricochetted into the sun, pawed for the sky, and let out a whinny that flared over the town.

Excited and glancing, the mare waited. For the first time, I saw the teaser, puny, and the reins. Flanks in a quiver, the stallion broke forward, closed, reared and plunged. Guiding in the reek and sweat flashed the red hand of the teaser. The stallion, straddled, pumped like his taut hamstrings must split. Then the teaser again, parting them, the spill passed on. The mare was led away. Snorting and champing, the chestnut was stalled.

Against the butt of a hobnailed boot, a farmer near me rapped his pipe.

—Well, boy, what d'ye make of it?

He grinned down over a porter belly.

Flushed and floundering, I left.

Every Monday I escaped to the yard. McElwaine was always there. And a few others I knew in school. Here we never spoke. Singly, privately, we awaited each loud unbolting and the rush that followed. It was like watching the start of the world.

Curried and ribboned and bobbed, the stallion roiled my dreams.

I saw the future: fifty-two Mondays bright and luscious in the year.

On my fourth visit, Lil Carroll, ladling sugar into two-pound bags, looked out a spidery window, saw me criminal among the men. And told.

When Mother called I was eating in the kitchen.

—Come up here you.

Fearful, I rose and followed her up to the parlour.

First she stood with her back to me, staring out on the flower-garden, said nothing. Then she turned, making a slow sign of the cross, and met me with a dead face.

—Where were you this afternoon?

—Playing football.

—Football! she mocked, in Carroll's yard?

I eyed the garden behind her.
—May, she said, Our Lady's month.
I shrank to a culprit.
—If I ever hear of you being there again, you'll get a dose you won't forget.
—Promise, she commanded, come on.
—I promise.
There was a pause while she studied me, and with it I could feel driving between us the fury of the yard, the glare and the ripeness, the sling of that door's opening, the stallion loosed again.
—Go back to your tea.
I left the room.
—Stallions, I heard her say on my way down the hall.

The Great Sword

Where Syl Jameson came from, no man knew: where bound for was revealed to me alone.

Jesus Christ on a motorbike, Tom Long, the ganger, named him when he arrived that Friday morning and was taken on in Cranston's Garage. No other way of describing Syl with the long blonde hair flying, bulbed forehead, blazing eyes, and bony narrowing cheeks, mouth, jaw — tearing up the street on a broken-winded autocycle, heading for some job that must be done or the world was at an end.

That was an arrival. About ten o'clock, the sun eating its way up the steely June sky, he soared out of himself.

—Lazarus, come forth, Mick Carson bawled as Syl was passing.

Mick's pin-head sticking up from a trench in Wolfe Tone Street, where he and a few more were fixing a leak in the main.

The men laughed. About thirty yards up, Syl wheeled and came back, cruising, the autocycle whining and sputtering. And for ten minutes he cruised up and down while Mick and the gang sank lower and lower into the trench, and bullets from Syl's blazing eyes rang above their heads. Eventually, the machine slowing almost to a stop, Syl cried out, over the sputtering engine, over the trench, over the opening windows and the opening doors, cried out in his northern accent — *Woe to the mockers* — the men flattened — *for their eyes are needles. But the eye of a needle awaits them — at the Gate* — the engine revved suddenly and hummed low again — *the Gate through which they shall not pass.* The engine revived, maintained power, and this time bore Syl away.

—Is he a Protestant? my mother asked, or what?

He was religion-mad, a story flew, had been through, *seen* through, the Church of Ireland, the Presbyterians, the Methodists, the Lutherans, the Witnesses, and the Salvation Army.

At noon I was in Cranston's Garage, that draughty shambles. Storm or calm, the wooden walls rippled and whinged. Only the banked odour of oil and grease supported the roof. Light, soon as it entered the place, fell down and died among the rusting machine-parts which grew from the dirt floor. Albert Cranston met me.

—You're not the first, Albert said, flinging a spanner aside — rattling a wall from end to end. Go on home. He's gone to his grub.

Albert. A long October briar, his face a berry that would never ripen.

—Stay clear of him, Albert warned, he's trapped lightning, boy, that's what he is.

He went down the garage and dropped, groaning, into a pit.

Two o'clock or half-past, and Syl was news again.

—You've great hands on you, Father John Donegan said to him.

Syl had just finished a tidy piece of work on the engine of the priest's car.

—A great pair of hands.

Rubbing his hands with a rag, Syl stared him.

—All things are possible, said Syl, don't you know that yourself?

He lowered the bonnet, tightened it. A gay secret ran out of the corners of his eyes and down over his face.

It was Syl's expression, Albert said, upset the priest.

—*All* things?

—All things, said Syl, all things, that's right — all.

I see, Father John, shoulders chuckling — that was his danger sign — came back, then I suppose that if —

—Take the word, take that word *all*.

Syl's jaw stuck out. And his right hand. Father John looked at it. Scarred. Colour of grease and oil.

—No, go on — more friendly —take it, take it.

Doubtful, Father John — nod of his head — took the word.

—Right, Syl went on, right. Now — try and surround it.

Father John scowled.

—Try it, Syl leaning against the priest's car, smiles up and down his face jigging encouragement. Go on. Try and surround the word *all*. Go on, try it.

So Father John, nettly, took on to surround the word (—Good, good, give it the try, Syl kept shoving in), circling it and squaring it and God knows what until he was light in the head. He huffed then, and tried to barge his way out by saying that whether you could or you couldn't, it didn't follow this and you couldn't claim that and in any case —

—Have you it surrounded yet? says Syl, on hunkers now, very patient, watching the floor.

Father John, ears turning white, started another palaver about logically speaking, and as far as he was taught —

—Have you it surrounded yet?

Knotting his mouth, Father John glared across at Albert.

—The wee word, says Syl, laughing to himself, the wee word *all*.

Poor Albert, paralysed, not knowing whether he was the middle of the week or maybe the end of it.

—I'm not used, Father John takes out the big stick, to being spoken to in —

—You haven't surrounded it, Syl rose like a salmon, and lit on him, and you won't, and will I tell you why?

Shouting, quivery with joy. Father John moved back.

—Because it's limitless, man, says Syl, arms wide, including Albert, including everybody, there's no bound to it, none, my God, when you think what's possible — Albert thought Syl would go up in flames but instead he held out his hand, the hand trembled, and the three of them stared at his palm — Nothing's impossible once you get inside that — spaceship, the hand bobbled gently, they all stared again. Look at it, will you, Syl sang, and look at it well because there I'm telling you is my spaceship — his voice dropped to a faraway croon that gurgled down to his toes — the wee, lovely, limitless word — *all*.

He floated out on to the street. The autocycle crackled. They heard him whine down the road.

Everyone had it in half-an-hour, and the procession started to

Cranston's. But Syl couldn't be found.

—Out on jobs, Albert said, and no more.

The afternoon sizzled. At four o'clock he cleared the congregation, twenty of us, idlers, chancers, gawky roamers. We stood outside awhile, and the rumour was that Syl had gone and joined the Dippers — a noisy sect in which, we understood, every man was his own Bishop — and was, at this moment, addressing them in the Meeting-house on Carrickgorman Hill. The Dummy Rogers said No, he was fixing a churn in the creamery. Vinny Gunn said he was in the Barracks on a charge of disturbing the peace.

They were all wrong. He was in our kitchen repairing the electric pump which had bested my father, Albert, and a dozen handymen over the previous three weeks. I was home at half-four and found him there. The housekeeper had let him in and then fled to an upstairs room.

—You're a Collins man, said Syl when I walked in and met my unbelievable luck. He glanced at the picture of General Michael Collins, green-and-gold against a background of cloud blue, Commander-in-Chief, National Army, which hung on the wall beside the window.

I told him Yes, I was a Collins man.

Crouched in the corner beside the sink, hands weaving over the pump, he smiled, and asked me what I thought of Collins.

—He was a great one, Syl.

Soundlessly, I settled on a chair.

—The greatest, he corrected, the greatest ever lived.

We looked at each other. We looked at the Collins picture. And there in the kitchen that smelled of turf kept in a tea-chest and dishcloths the housekeeper had boiling on the stove, Syl opened for me his bag of dreams.

All things were possible, he said. He himself had heard, for example, the Voice Within and the Voice Beyond. He explained how he had heard them, what they had said, and 'the meaning thereof'. He led me into the Cycle of Numbers — seven was his number and he'd been born under the sign of the Lion. Truth was the Ocean, Syl told me — *I can prove it*. He did, and then, closing his eyes, went on to demonstrate the Link between all things. Gob open wide as the mouth of the Shannon, I sat on the edge of my arse, hypnotised — but he hadn't even begun. He laid bare the

Compass of the Pyramids and the Greater Compass buried beneath the floors of the Amazon Jungle, unravelled the Black Art and the White, indicated what might be taken from the Koran and what discarded, described how Time opens and Time shuts, gave me the secret of Dominion over the Elements and the Rule of Animals, quoted scripture, quoted poetry, quoted the Three Lost Prophecies of Malachy the Thin, and — the sun reaching down to stack the kitchen with spears of gold, a glister of sweat sitting like chain-mail on his forehead — asked me if I knew he'd held the Great Sword in his hand.

—No, Syl, I whispered.

—I stood alone on the Ridge of the World, said Syl, looking past me — through the door that led into the hall, and I held the Great Sword of Light, not by the blade either — any eejit could do that — but by the handle, boy, the handle.

His hands clenched. And bronze ran in the whites of his eyes. It was a blinding flame, he said, that scorched the hearts of the unworthy but he had looked at it and into it without harm.

—He knew all that, suddenly he switched — the Collins picture, he held the Great Sword.

Anger skewered Syl's face.

— Which was why, he added, they struck him down.

From my chair by the door I nodded. And waited for what he would now say. He was coming to something very important. The sunlight had stopped moving, the spears. Syl's eyes swung to the edge of his forehead, lay there, glinting, flickered round corners, flew back to their burning nests.

—There'll be another Great One soon, he said, another Coming. Did you know that?

Lungs daring me to breathe, I shook my head.

—Well, there will — again his eyes swung and glinted and flickered round corners and came home pleased — This could be a great wee country, he said, if it was one, if it was made whole.

My lips fluttered.

—Another Great One, said Syl, it's written.

—Who, Syl? I asked, who'll it be?

He examined me. Alight. Circles formed about his mouth, smiles, tipping nose and chin as they began to move. He seemed perched on air. God, I thought, don't let him float away on me, don't, please. The circles were spreading, the ripple of smiles,

Syl bobbing.

—Who, Syl? I swayed a dry tongue, who'll it be?

He opened his mouth to answer, and the housekeeper — curse her — clattered something upstairs. Straightaway he was on his feet, that was it, gathering wrenches and spanners and washers and grommets and oilrags. He clicked a lever. The pump buzzed and burred, and burred steadily.

—Good-luck, boy.

He was at the door.

—Good-bye, Syl, I said — flustered.

But I was right. I never saw him again. He didn't even report back to Cranston's. Down the avenue with him, and instead of turning right towards the town, he turned left. The main road north. Forty miles off was the Border. The hedge hid him now. I listened. Somewhere inside the racket of the autocycle bugles began to twirl and spit, and a black cackle of rooks rose. In awe I watched, and Syl swept into sight on Hourican's Brae, wheels flaking on the rise. I watched him grow as he climbed the brae, unwind his bones and shed his span until, treetops his runway, he hit the skyline. For an instant he hung there — blonde hair silk on the wind.

—Syl, I shouted, Syl, Syl, Syl, and, my head spinning, I saw the sun — green-gold, blue cloud beyond — stand up on its hind legs to watch him on his way.

Willie Wynne, Con Moto

When the *Lyric* was built in the early 'forties, it was fashionable for a time to go there at least once a week. The *best* people, the Parish Priest, the doctors, the solicitors, the Garda Superintendent, well-to-do shopkeepers (include wives, *embonpoint* and featly girdled, in all cases above except the initial one) inhabited the carmine plush area at the rear. They were, collectively, the 1/8s. Next, dun and not so plush, the 1/3s: those who were progressing, factory operatives doing well on overtime, shophands able to put by a bit, a variety of clerks, mechanics, and a few restrained couples saving their pennies and their passion for the day when. Beyond these, on wooden benches, and right to the *Modigliani* angles below the screen, the rabble hived, the 9ds: direct labourers, rags-bottles-and-bones men, demireps, idlers, simpletons, that echelon which had not yet shuffled off the Workhouse past — inheritance rarely spoken of precisely because its suppurating reality was so hard to deny.

There was, of course, a degree of infiltration — but minor. Occasionally, some clerk, exulting in a festal bonus, invaded the 1/8s, received the murky rebuffs of the *élite*. Or one of the rabble might advance to the intermediate zone, there to sit — brassy reminder that it was a slithery world, that, neutrality or no, Europe's rumble-tumble might easily be here in the morning, and then what? Such anomalies only emphasized that the *Lyric* was an arena in which social divisions were jaggedly defined. Yet, in the *Lyric*, more than anywhere else, these same divisions were open invitingly to attack.

The night on which this was most memorably demonstrated was an — otherwise — ordinary night at the cinema. There was a fair attendance except for the 9ds, it was Thursday and the week's expenditure had diminished patrons in that area so that the corral geometry of the benches enclosed no more than half-a-dozen people. The programme scheduled was pleasantly humdrum. Without mishap, it unreeled to a Travel Feature (pre-war, cheap), regular interlude item between the 'short' and the main offering. As always, this was a sunny presentation, Mediterranean or Caribbean, enhanced by tawny beings who trod the littoral as if they had just emerged, full-formed, from the fluid ivory-yellow sand. For variety, the cameras sometimes moved inland to ramble the mountains, approving — with a *schwarmerei* that barely escaped self-parody — the 'quaint' and the 'timeless'. The effect was to introduce a well-being quite unadulterated by yearning, since these havens had, for the moment — the panzers, the U-boats — been translated to the regions of the purely mythical.

The cameras had, in fact, taken to the mountains — the *Lyric*'s masked sidelights contributing a melon hush of comfort, tobacco smoke hanging like an abstract of *Relaxation* — when the background music picked on a tune familiar to everybody, *The Donkey Serenade*. If it was familiar to all, it was particularly the possession of the 1/8s. The piece had *ton* — part rhythm and part the macaronic flavour of the ditty, was distinct from the rag-bag traffic of the day. Further, it was aureoled by the courtly gesturing of Nelson Eddy and Jeanette McDonald, and thus gained an orphic beat. The 1/3s were in touch also but in a ruminant sort of way. Because their radios chanted eighteen hours of the twenty-four, the 9ds knew it well. They could be expected to revere it or shit on it according to their humour.

As the opening bars flicked off the soundtrack, there was a susurrus of pleasure, succeeded by an impulse to join in, lilting, humming, any accompaniment but some, *some*: then — shift of feeling almost audible — the impulse was choked. Good breeding won, you didn't lilt or hum or whistle in these circumstances, you contained yourself, listened, allowed others to enjoy. Even the 9ds behaved . . . *Dum-tee, dum-tee dee-dum dum-tee, dum-dee, dum-dum* . . . Mrs Cyril McGovern, wife to the State Solicitor for the county, tapped her foot noiselessly and smiled. The mountains. The quaint village. Old man, jennet, pannier . . . *Dum-tee, dum-tee dee-dum dum-tee, dum-dee, dum-dum* . . . Someone commenced to whistle. Bold liquid warbling that made the orchestra its servant on the spot, captured the melody, and capered on.

Susurrus again. No. Crepitation. Quick check in the mobile gloom to place the sound. It seemed to be coming from the 1/8s, left-hand side, middle. It was. Who? Knees propped, the *artiste* was humped down in his seat, just the head visible, blonde gipsy sheen, and the face, tilted, smoothly intent, highly manipulable lips purring with the sphincter legerdemain of your born *siffleur*. So it's you, said the 1/8s, averting from the smart of recognition. Willy Wynne, *con moto*, continued whistling.

The Wynnes lived in a street which hung raffishly off the bourgeois trunk of the town. They sold fruit all the time, and herrings now and then. The door of the small house was constantly open. A barrow stood by the footpath. Hurrying between house and barrow, you carried away the patchouli of orchards, grubby orchards, and a sourly teeming sea. The mother was a big woman, unrepentantly zigane, the father a whiny runt forever bossed by the barrow. The sons and daughters were freckled specimens, banana skin in pigment and psychology. Willy was nineteen.

Whistling. The opening strategy of the 1/8s was forecastable. No great philosophical insight was needed to tell them that if they didn't hear the whistling, then, in some sense, it ceased to be. They decided not to hear, entrenched instantly on this ground, and waited. The 1/3s were amused but uninvolved, the 9ds unconcerned: Rose Hand, dozing in a corner; the two wrinkled Tinleys, jockey-crouched, brooding on the afternoon's treacheries at the Curragh; three kids coughing over cigarettes. Indulging in a series of chromatic flourishes, vibrant and fluty, Willy led the orchestra into the primary theme . . . *Twee-twee-twee, twee-twee-twee, tu-reep tree* . . .

An extraordinarily dogged if brief tussle followed. The communal spirit of the 1/8s fought by every shift and deceit imaginable to deny the sound. They gave themselves to the screen, they gave themselves to fantasies of lust and profit, they adventured, potholing among caves of thought and feeling they rarely visited. And for a space it seemed possible they would win. Until Vin Tierney, grocer cantankerous, sclerotic, broke ranks — the Wynnes owed him £75 — and let fly a phosphorescent dart of hostility in Willy's direction. That was it. One by one, then all at once, the 1/8s succumbed. No longer any question: Willy Wynne, gay caballero, was whistling.

The whistling, if you could be objective about it, *had* something winning — a fresh *toccata* exuberance which derived, in fact, from the ten-and-sixpence Willy had won at pitch-and-toss earlier in the evening. Further, the acoustics of the *Lyric*, usually recalcitrant, seemed to delight in the unexpected sound. Roof and wall took it in flight, put a shine on, let it loose again. *Toccata* it flew. Innocent in a way. So it might have remained — had not Willy's capillaries interpreted accurately, and at speed, the mood of his immediate audience. He looked about him and confirmed. Minutely, the whistling altered.

Meanwhile, the 1/8s, recovering from the shock and propelled by a vehemence which surprised them, were binding to an opposition. As they joined, there was still the infantile shrugging hope that this might not have to be suffered after all . . . *Sweet-sweet-sweet, too-eee-too, tweet* . . . No, apparently it must. Traveller on the listening faces now a *risus* flicker that boded trouble, Do you mind, Mister Wynne? We'd prefer the orchestra unaccompanied. Ascending chirrupy cadences. *Pup.* So you can whistle! A run of trills pinked and pinged, frolic of self-discovery, accomplishment, and (oh, you bastard, Willy) the lick of power.

He had, indeed, just glimpsed the delicate ferocity of the weapon he held. The natural *brio* of his beginning had early taken on the tinge of malice but the incipient, even premature, writhing of the enemy extended his vision dramatically. For an instant, he was Lenin. If his followers in the far benches were still dormant, the revolutionary lives with that — and Willy would. They'd come; the 1/3s didn't matter; the opposition were here. Luminous with exultation, he waltzed up the scale, inspected the field from high C, and then — no comment — glided to a prolonged, contemplative, and subtly teasing A . . .

Either panicked by that or operating inside a rhythm which governs all such situations, the 1/8s made a common and debilitating blunder. Bob Geary of the Bank and one or two others had glanced back at Father Terry Walsh to see how he was taking it. Noting the glances, Father Terry hesitated, half-stood up, and glared, prognathous, unambiguous, at the offender. The adjacent rows quickly contributed supporting scowls. Mounted, however, from behind, and ameliorated by the dimness, the attack faltered, lost its way, ultimately grew ashamed of itself, and expired among matchboxes, cigarette-ends, and sweet-papers. Father Terry — thump of the seat — sat down.

Too-eee-twee, whit-too-ee, sweet-sweet-sweet-whit too-eee too-eee twee . . . What was to be done? Nobody knew? Skin wriggled as the silence built around a spiral of prickly twitters. No one looking at Willy. Came a low chuckle from the 1/3s, and it was left to Doc Markey — who had a tongue — to introduce the next stage. Beyond patience, *Little shite*, said the Doc. Cinema-whisper. Willy paused as the 1/8s rallied, dropped a crotchet — rudely, and skittered after the tune again unsubdued.

War now, by God! The impact of the Doc's comment and Willy's reply was to clarify — and to blur. For a second, as if raised on a swivel-chair, the criminal was visible and his malevolent intentions but, immediately, he disappeared in a visceral tangle which included Fair Day rows, St Vincent de Paul, Jeanette McDonald, England, the cosy funnel of motes linking the projection-room and the screen, *graffiti* in certain parts of the Workhouse ruin, each item peculiarly vivid despite (or because of) this dusk which had spawned them all. And the slick of Willy's hair. Little shite.

Amigo mio, does she not have a dainty bray? They surveyed him again, eyes on all sides snapping. Tilted face greased by the half-light, finicky spewing lips. Humping himself further into the seat, hands pocketed, legs crossed, God, wouldn't you love to give him one good — but there was a second marauder: the incorrigible safety of the brat. You could hardly clout him. Even threaten. Not here. Not anywhere. And well he knew it . . . *She listens carefully to each little tune you play* . . . Titters from the 1/3s.

Willy — measuring developments — could see Hubert Lynch, the Mrs, the two sonsy daughters, tearing at him, small dog's teeth sharp in the whites of their eyes. Grand. But it was time, wasn't it? his followers showed themselves. The mere wish was charismatic.

Tootle-tootle-tootle-tee.

The 9ds were in! It was Rose Hand — *La Bella Senorita* — hers the contrapuntal support. The building seemed to shake itself, prepare for possibilities undreamt of; either in relief or apprehension the murk lightened, and Willy, elated, razzle-dazzled the melody through a narrowing bore, silver and intense. Jaysus, this was marvellous —

—Do you mind?

In this squeeze of agony for the 1/8s, Superintendent Paul Boyle was the man who dared. He was in the same row as Willy, four seats distant, no one between to dilute the archangel tolerance of the voice.

—Do you mind?

Willy's head turned — eyelids dropping an immaculate synchronism — spouted a few metallic chirps into the Superintendent's face, found its tranced jubilant slant again. *Accelerando* twirls. The Superintendent sat back in his seat, stared gaunt ahead. *Si, si, me muchachito!* Snapping eyes switched, bit blindly at the screen, mountains, faraway village, old man, jennet, pannier.

Led by Rose, the 9ds had wheeled, and now sat poised, six surprised sailors manning the itchy guns of a new Potemkin. At their backs the screen mimed irrelevantly. Timid rustle through the 1/3s. The 1/8s poisonously still. And, with the authority of one who has outstripped fallibility, Willy accepted the mandate. Feckless of the melody, the whistling abruptly soared so that the performer appeared to gain a position on one of the brute girders which braced the roof. That achieved, the spectacular piping was split by a scolding note, sub-song, modulated jeer that was blasphemously maintained.

The 1/8s winced — but kept control. Assuming the masochistic rigidity of the about-to-be-martyred, they watched the screen. That is, they watched what they could see of it because — events moving with the impetus of anarchy — the 9ds were already standing on the benches, gesticulating enthusiasm, and more clamorous by the second. Still, in gross concert, the 1/8s watched, endured that raucous untutored ballet, endured the insulting spew of sound from the inviolable girders, the murk above.

It was at this point the 1/3s wheeled, sober, imitative, but at once sucked into the rhythm of revolt. From aloft — slouched despotically in the seat, Willy could barely be seen — there was no let-up, the jeer more venomous. Above the rumpus, a shower was heard hitting the roof of the *Lyric*, running in sloppy waves on the resonant galvanize.

Who was first to the sequent image will never be known. Just before Rose shouted, Mona Coyle — the Poultry Instructress — found her left hand flipping to her face in a pathetically protective gesture. And there may have been others, anticipant and quailing. What Rose shouted into the excitement was — *Piss on them, bhoy!*

That many of the 1/3s had been suborned was indicated by the extra loud roar which met the suggestion. The marmoreal fixity of the 1/8s spasmed, awesomely held. For the last time, the whistling altered. Instantly, Rose rapped her ranks to silence. Willy, continuing, no doubt, his search for low-slung comfort, had passed out of sight (one knee *did* show, a disconnected shine) but from the dark overhead the whistling came, flighted parabolically in the main yet with quirky variations, watery overtones, and, blooming in the slipstream, a cloacal breath that registered as the sportive afterthought of pure genius.

To their terrible stillness the 1/8s held. By the time the Manager arrived it was all over.

Gunning's Word

We are dice in the hands of God the Gambler — there's not a doubt of it. Is any man safe? Look what happened to little Paul Pritchard: Paul made one slip — and he'd had it. He went down to Neligan's this grand summer evening to arrange with Frank about the canopy-bearers for Thursday's procession, and who should be there but Gunning.

—Paul himself, fresh from Damascus, Gunning opened, name your poison, Paul.

—Not now, Mick, thanks, Paul shied towards the door, just came in to —

—What's seldom is wonderful, Paul. Advancing, Gunning swept him amiably forward and on to a stool by the counter. Now, name your poison.

—Bitter lemon, said Paul.

—May it run through you, Gunning grinned and ordered a double Irish for himself.

Gunning was the region's champion boozer. The curious thing was that he seemed to thrive on dissipation. True, he'd yielded most of his innards to the surgeons, true he'd wrecked a good law practice, and true he'd driven the wife to an early old age. Gunning, however, was still there, in funds, and blooming. Everyone preached at him but it was pointless. Gunning — petting the immaculate handkerchief in the immaculate breast-pocket of the immaculate suit — would remark —

—Resilient class of an evening, don't you think?

Gunning's favourite word: resilient.

Meanwhile, conversation was proceeding. Or, rather, Gunning was. Paul sat above the bitter lemon and listened to the usual tale of another evening on the batter. Gunning had gone into the city to a dog-meet, met so-and-so — a trainer, got a tenner on a tasty outsider, then off about midnight to the trainer's headquarters where they'd christened — as far as he could remember — a newborn bitch, best of breeding, with champagne, then retired to the trainer's house where there was a party going on, et cetera, et cetera...

—Sounds like a great romp, said Paul.

—It was a kind of a Tercentenary Waxies' Dargle, Paul, Gunning gave the nod for another double, a Tercentenary Waxies' Dargle.

Paul said nothing.

—Well, and how're things with you, tell me, Gunning enquired, still piling up the shekels, I expect?

—Mick, Paul put down the bitter lemon, will you tell me something?

—Of course.

—Did it ever occur to you to kick the bottle out of your life?

—Often, Paul, often, but with the assistance of my good guardian angel, I was always able to put the —

—For God's sake, Mick, Paul seemed suddenly reduced to two brightly honed cheek-bones, cut out the balderdash.

And didn't he blitz Gunning. Disgrace to his home, to his profession, to the town, time he got some sense, a man of his age, but he'd listen to no one, all right, nobody else mattered but if nothing else would stop him, you'd imagine he might have some regard for his own health, that last hospital session had been damn nearly *it*, the town, as a matter of fact, had given him up for dead, and what about the next trip, no man's health could stand that pace, his couldn't stand it, nor would it, and he, Paul, wasn't a bit afraid to say to his face what was being said all over.

—There's a coffin booked for you, Mick, he jabbed a finger at Gunning, kept jabbing it, he'd worked himself into what, for Paul, was a hell of a state. If you don't lay off you've a year, maybe eighteen months — and don't say — still jabbing — don't say you weren't told.

The barman was waiting for Gunning to come out with it —

—Resilient class of an evening, don't you think?

It didn't come. Instead, Gunning studied Paul who, jabbing finger recalled to base, was catching his breath, and —

—I'll bury *you*, Paul, said Gunning, his smile the smile of one who has been granted a rare illumination, I'll bury you, boy.
Paul looked at him.
—I, said Gunning, will — bury — you.

Fair enough. It gave Paul a slight dunt at the time but why make a fuss over a thing like that? He put it out of his mind. And yet the next time he saw Gunning — it was on the street — he'd willingly have turned back or whipped over to the other footpath only, of course, it would have been barefaced. Bracing himself, he kept going, just *Nice day, Mick*, he wouldn't stop, lick by, and —
—Day, Mick.
—Paul —
Gunning's arm barred the way.
—Paul, said Gunning with a smile, I'll bury you.
And moved on.
There you have the commencement exercises. They met, say, five times in the following weeks. Each time, as it happened, there was company. And, each time, Gunning delivered his good-natured warning, loudly, so's all could hear.
—Paul, I'll bury you.
—No bother to you, Mick. No one I'd rather have do it.
Paul carried it off fairly well but he felt that bringing the thing into the public arena was a bit much.

It was the wife, a few weeks later, who noticed him going into himself. Turning mopey. Especially in the evenings.
—What's wrong with you?
—Nothing.
Something at that last meeting of the Knights?
—What are you talking about?
—Or is it the business?
—Business was never better, thank God.
—What's up with you, then?
—Nothing.
A day or two later he told her. He'd come home from a removal of remains where, in spite of precautions, he'd bumped into Gunning, there'd been another exchange, and . . . he told her the whole story.
—Well, you're all babies, I know, the wife gazed on him in

wonder, but this is the livin' limit.

—I know, said Paul, it's stupid. I know that.

—And so this, she hadn't taken her gaze off him, is what you're mopey about?

—I wouldn't mind if he hadn't made it public.

—Shure what difference does —

—I don't like being made a spectacle. By a sot.

—But, dear, it's all in your own mind, don't —

—It's not all in my own mind. I told you it's public.

—Don't be worrying about it, just put the whole nonsense out of your head.

It was about half-nine. She fixed up his jar, and put him to bed early.

—All you want to do is relax, she told him, you work too hard anyway.

The very next day, didn't she pay a call on Maura Gunning, took her courage in her hands, and explained the whole thing. Mick obviously meant no harm but she was afraid it was getting in on Paul, she might be mistaken, the children were all away now, nest empty, and, no doubt, men also went through a change of life in their own peculiar fashion but, anyway, would Maura, if she could, drop a word, discreetly . . .

—To be sure, I will, Maura was a good sort, he doesn't pay much attention to me but I'll see what can be done.

That was Tuesday. Friday afternoon, Paul was flicking through invoices in the office at the rear of the shop when he heard steps, looked up, and there was Gunning.

—Well, Mick?

Gunning, strangely solemn, hesitated in the doorway. He was wearing a black hat which Paul didn't recollect having seen on him before.

—What can I do for you?

If Gunning had said what he usually said, Paul — on home ground — might conceivably have gone for him. But Gunning didn't.

—Paul, he stepped into the office, you know that little game we've been playing?

—Yes.

—Listen, Gunning looked earnestly at the floor, looked up,

continued, it was only a game, Paul. In other words, when I said — what I said — I didn't mean it, Paul, you understand that?

Paul, looking helplessly into Gunning's large grey eyes, might have nodded, he couldn't afterwards be sure.

—Shake, said Gunning.

Paul stuck out a hand. It was taken in a powerful grip. Gunning left.

And, under a skin of sweat, Paul deduced instantly what had happened. He waited until the shop closed at six, and a further half-hour until the staff had gone. Then he went upstairs, confronted the wife, and ballyragged her from attic to cellar. It was their first row in thirty years of marriage.

The moping continued but the wife didn't realise how serious the situation was until she opened a letter of his by mistake one morning a month later, and discovered a doctor's bill. Ten guineas, a consultation fee, and it was from a well-known heart-man in the city. The date clicked. Paul had been to the city that day — business trip. She presented it to him at lunch.

—What, pray God, is this?

He looked at it.

—So?

—Shure you have no heart trouble?

—It was just a check.

—A check? And you haven't lost a day in bed as long as I've known you?

—I know that.

—And he said your heart was fine?

—That's right.

She didn't pursue the matter but, that evening, she got him into the car, and they drove twenty miles to her cousin, a GP, and, incidentally, a first-class man. He examined Paul top to bottom, and gave his verdict. Not a thing wrong except nerves. Paul was, to put it simply, het-up.

—You've been too hard at it, Paul, he told him, rest far more. You're not an old man but you're not a young man either. My advice to you is a month's holiday, two months if you can spare it.

—The heart *is* fine, Michael, the wife asked, he was inclined to get —

—The heart is fine — and will remain fine — so long as he

relaxes. If he doesn't, I make no promises.
—Thanks, Michael, said Paul, and, thank-you, dear, he added as — looking neither left nor right — he led her towards the car.

The cousin could have told them, there and then, exactly how it would go but he wasn't being paid for that. They took three weeks on the continent, a super-charged tour which fitted in Lourdes, Fatima, the Belgian shrine at what's-its-name, and four 'Great Cathedrals' for good measure. Paul came home fatigued and jittery, resumed work, took to drinking — upstairs cupboard drinking — and six months later was on the flat of his back with *angina*. He's on his feet again now but you wouldn't bet on his lasting. The general opinion is a year, eighteen months at the outside.

So there it is. Do he and Gunning ever meet? Frequently. Does Gunning ever say, well, what he used to say? Christ, no. On the contrary, he tells Paul that he's looking extraordinarily well. And, nothing if not humane, makes sombre references to another hospital trip which — doctor's insistence — he's got lined up for himself in the near future. In the bars, Gunning's judgement is that Paul 'lacked resilience'.

—He was never what you'd call a very resilient class of a man now, was he? Gunning will enquire, raising his glass of the (undiluted) hard, I certainly would never have used that word of him.

Naturally, the bars concur.

An Aspect of the Rising

Opposite Adam and Eve's, the up-river east wind that would frizzle a mermaid's fins a zephyr tickle the second I sighted her. Plump chiaroscuro: black bobbed hair, white cheeks, black coat, white calves, black shoes, high-heeling along the far footpath. She looked recklessly like herself, in her wisdom gazed neither to the left nor to the right but let the plastic bag winking on her rump com'ither me through the scooting traffic and urgent to her side.
   —We're in business, I matched her step, leaned toward her, eager as a guitar.
   —Fast from the trap, aren't you, she spoke from the lips out, never slackened pace, wonder you weren't made ointment of crossing the street.
   —You're beautiful, pursuing I ladled compliments into her small skintight ear, and now she coyed. The black pencilled line above her visible eye, the right, took my admiration. Oblique but eloquent of the horizontal, a masterpiece. Still we hurried.
   —Where're we going?
   —You have a car?
   Had a car.
   —I have to have a cup of coffee, her mauve mouth belonged to the first woman, the destined rib, you can get the car. And wait for me up here outside The Last Post.
   She went. Captive, I watched her buttocks acclaim a royal leaving. Her scent stayed. A firm scent. And ready. Appled. That was it. Apples and muscles. Taffeta flashing above her bright-bare calves, the door of The Last Post opened before her.

   Philomena, she introduced herself. And my instinct, I decided, had been sound. Anything with ears on it bar a pot is the rule along the river most nights but here was a real professional, her every motion *credo*.

—How're they hanging? she enquired as we drove off towards Kingsbridge and the Park beyond.

—Two eggs in a hanky.

Chuckling, she produced cigarettes, lit two, and passed one to me. They were Polish and smuggled — a sailor from Riga.

—Poles, I say to him, she reminisced, settling back in the seat, knees sudden and vocal as the skirt rose, poles is right.

Sure of your wares is sure of your stares. Philomena, slowly, fingered open her coat, and — I glanced across — the wares, big unbiddable breasts, trim belly, and roomy thighs, began to move and converse under blouse and skirt as if equally sure of themselves. To the silencer in these excitements I bowed. She, reading me with black eyes, understood, and, leaning over, petted my abundant crotch. Jesus, I thought, giddy, I'll have to be dug out of her. The last buses were being shunted home, on the roof of the Brewery a bouncy moon. Apples and the contraband of the Baltic odorous about us, we took the hill, sped through the gates and into the Park.

—Here, Philomena?

A few hundred yards in, and impetuous, I was steering for a convenient nest under the adjacent and glooming trees.

—No, keep going. Right. Keep going. There's a little spot I know. I'll show you the way.

Venue. Between friends, I asked, what was the difference, here or there? No good. We drove. Insistent, she directed me, her neat coaxing hand slipping in and out of the light.

—It's a special spot I have. Not far.

On reflection, I yielded. She was right. Not any hole in the wall but a sanctified lair. What a woman! We passed the Zoo. A lion raged within, and down to our right flamingoes fluttered and gossiped in the pink insomnia of their watery beds.

—The Zoo's grand, she voiced dreamily, keep going.

Open spaces, right, left, this fork now, trees, silver choppy in the branches, no trees, silver seamless along the grass. Delay's a randy foreman. I glimpsed the dank remains of turfstacks which had warmed Dublin winters ago, I glimpsed the long-legged ghosts of slaughtered deer but I thought neither of the huddled fire nor the red jittery stag. She sat there, relaxed, substantial in the run of shadows, now and then nibbling my neck.

—Nearly there.

—Christ, I grouched, we'll be at the Boyne before we know it.

Next moment — Here, she pointed, left.

And, it wasn't just the voice, curiously level, I felt — alteration. On the turn, I inspected her. Sure enough, she was tight in the seat, tight as Christy's britches. Suspicion cranked me. No, I calmed myself. The cramp of an instant. It means nothing. We were driving towards a stand of fir and pine a hundred yards away, a large building visible in fragmented outline beyond. Deep into the trees, I pulled up. Philomena, my new Philomena, was out of the car, wordless, before I'd switched off the ignition. Worried, I followed.

Smell of the trees. And the place's seasoned privacy. And the midnight dusk. There she was — a stranger and grim — her back to a young fir a few yards off. What was she at? Climbing the palisade of her remove, I advanced. Rhinestones flickered but didn't beckon. I was beside her, whispering. Weep for my whispers. She was wood against that tree. My fingers implored. Colder than wood.

—What's wrong?

Two bleak eyes, she stood there. I made a rude remark. It passed lightly through her — your hand through a ghost.

—What is it? I tried again, what's wrong?

Useless. I scanned her face, a hunter's face, stalking what? Wind skidded on the branches. Philomena and I waited. For five stinging seconds, and then the spurs of a mean anger raked me. Let me omit the vituperation I flung upon her. It shames my balls, and it balls my shame. Tranced black and white in a shaft of the moon, she paid, thank God, no heed. I wheeled to depart, and not three steps had I taken when the woman, catspitting, was soaring to her singular and sainted glory.

—You crawthumpin' get of a Spaniard that never was seen — incredulous I stopped: the wood rang — with your long features and your long memory and two and twenty-two strings to your bow, what crooked eggs without yolks are you hatching between rosaries tonight?

Birds racketing. The Spaniard? To a skelp of joy, I connected. The building beyond — Áras an Uachtaráin, De Valera himself under sharp and sharpening fire.

—Diagrams, I heard — and a sneer bisected the word as it flew, more of them you're amusing yourself with maybe, proving that A is B and B is C and a Republic is Jaysus knows what until Euclid himself'd be cracked in Dundrum trying to make you't. But, Professor Isosceles — she drew harsh breath, raced on, discovering the beat of her scorn — it was damn all diagrams or anything else we got from you above in Boland's Mills when Simon Donnelly had to take over the command, you sitting there with your heart in your gob and your arse in a sling.

Listen to me. There are sights you never forget. Her face wild, throat wilder, hands two kicking lanterns, knees ivory below — immobile and smooth, Philomena roasted the Long Fellow. Practice graced her, rancours unnameable and a fury of the bones powered her — she left nothing out, there was nothing she didn't fit in: the Treaty, the Civil War, the Oath, the Hangings of the 40s, Emigration, Inflation, Taxation, the Language, the lot. An eighth of a mile away, brooding or at his prayers, His Excellency heard not a word but, chosen by the Gods, I heard, the ground heard and the wind and the sky's cupped ear. We listened to that alto scurrility leap the air, listened in ecstasy and heard — reaches distant — backlane and gutter answer, stir, shift, and jig maddened to an old, a blithe, a bitter tune.

—You, she cried aloud and aloft, you long spear in the side of a Christian people, may God drop a clog on you, may the Divil make a knot of you, may coals scorch you and may cinders choke you, may smoke annoy you and may soot destroy you, may the day peel your skins and the night screech your sins, may . . .

Don't ask me how long it lasted but bring back Moses and I'll say it to his teeth: she finished that diatribe a creature of flame. You'd kneel to her.

—You there, says she — there was barely a pause — into the shriven quiet, are you comin' or goin'?

I was dazzled but comin'. Gaily she murmured me in. Zips purred. The undergrowth lured. To it we went, and at it we stayed.

Birds settled again on the branches. In the great house beyond the trees — lights burning here and there, in the city below, and all over Ireland, medals were being dusted, ribbons spruced, orations polished and artillery oiled for the Fiftieth Anniversary of the Insurrection.

Boarding

On Thursday at three I stood before Clongowes. The barbered frontage, two-thirds ivied, shone even in the downpour. I sprinted the gravel, swung back the smooth-rolling oak door, and stepped inside. In the sparse light of the shallow hallway stone and iron, four teak doors, and a baroque Ignatius reaching for his sword.
 —You're the man come to meet Father Naughton?
 —Yes.
 The butler, skipping yield of a recess to the right.
 —This way. Desperate summer. Cows swimming on dry land these parts.
 No-age joker, small, ox-necked.
 —And haycocks sailing for the sea.
 A lift in his voice hoisted him aboard one, hoisted us both to the first landing, his dark jaw, dark livery, tangy with the salt of misrule.
 —This way now.
 We were rising into the body of the castle, up cranky stairs and along the porous silence of low windowless corridors. I recall: the broad back climbing, saints and martyrs in wood and plaster and great coughing canvases of the romantic decline, bags of shadow, the continuing ascent, still the broad back there a yard or two ahead but remote, the surround distancing us as it pleased.
 —Here you are, sir.
 A room opening to me.
 —He'll be with you shortly, sir.
 Sirs now.
 —And if there's anything you need, sir.

—Thank-you, sir.

In the room prayer and penance hung about like chewed bones. And what next under God, Ignatius, the Black Pope, and imminent Father Naughton? Minutes passed, and my hand drew open the drawer of a desk. A blotched page from an old handbook. Without moving it, I read —

HISTORICAL NOTES

- 1180 *Clongowes and Rathcoffey in the Mainham Estate of Adam de Hereford.*
- 1415 *Probable date of the first large castle.*
- 1493 *Clongowes formally granted to the Eustaces, Viscounts Baltinglass.*
- 1542 *Jesuits first came to Ireland.*
- 1641 *Eustaces of Clongowes join Confederate revolt.*
- 1642 *Clongowes Castle captured and demolished by troops of General Monk.*
- 1718 *Castle restored by Stephen Fitzwilliam Browne.*
- 1813 *Castle and Estate bought by the Jesuits.*

Shutting the drawer I stood there. And a bald little priest spun into the room as if a squadron jigged at his heels.

—Hello. How are you? You're very welcome — he engaged my hand, disposed of it — Sit down, won't you? Well now, the position is this.

Father Harold Naughton, SJ, tea-rose face fresh above the tended soutane and the laughing shoes, marched the room, and dealt me the stunning irrelevancies of the mighty.

—We have three-hundred boys in the place, he said on the swivel, teeth trifling with a smile, the cream of the country — rich and thick.

—We may ask you to teach anything, he said, rolling the balls of his feet, from Hebrew to Hindustani. It's the system. The Minister for Education is mad.

—This place *is* isolated, he said, looking out the window through his lips, but one suicide in a hundred and fifty years is fair enough, isn't it? In any case, he went on, I don't believe that was a suicide. The fool fell into the moat.

Ten minutes of a wet and blowy afternoon in that high room of the castle on the limestone plain. Pantried somewhere below, my supple guide; de Hereford and Eustace and Fitzwilliam Browne wild in the walls, Naughton speaking on, a trim survivor, a spirit — fire and steel — that sang as the bullet sings. And I knew the rummaging curiosity of youth about to seduce me.

—Great. Great — a short hand, polished at the joints was mine — Great. The population arrive on September 5th.

As I left, it had stopped raining but the light had not improved. The avenue's guard of limes, scent hesitantly lacing the murk, attended. Stillness. No activity but for a tall priest — in his left hand, stiffly, a slash-hook — crossing a field away to the right. Making for the woodland.

Next evening, I was back in Donegal, my lodgings the house of a butcher on a knot of rock above the sea. The butcher's wife was towelling my hair, talking once more of the life she'd known as a nurse in Glasgow, putting before me the images of her hunger and the excitements of her love.

The Hurt Mind

—The Boys who Beat the Black and Tans the Boys from the County Cork — not quite true, not quite true, what about Lord, what about Lord Doneraile and his bucks and his blades, I read books, what about the rights of the Big House, what about the seed and the breed of the carriage-and-four staring from the ditches at the carriage-and-four as the carriage-and-four swept by, I'm talking of the hurt mind, I'm talking of the hurt mind in wait and knowing as the hurt mind knows, the litter of the Big House and the scatter of Captain Buck and Major Blade, oh yes, and when the Tans came who's fighting who?, answer me that, the ditches fightin' their own, they're fightin' from the hurt mind, and by the bye what about the beagle hunt, *Come on Lord Doneraile* — I read this in a book, I read two books a year and I read them well and one of them had this: Fine day for a hunt, right, take a fresh young slip of a one never touched, strip and rub all over with aniseed oil — three scents for the beagle, hare, red herrin', aniseed oil — strip to the pelt and rub all over and let loose, a fair start, if it's a hunt a hunt let it be, she'll travel, she's young and supple and she's layin' a trail and the day's long, now your beagles, now the Lord, now Captain Buck and Major Blade, the beagles sniffin', there's a sight for you — three scents for the beagle, hare, red herrin', aniseed oil — they've picked her scent, they've a trail, we're away, north with her, south with her, east with her, west with her, wasting her time and she knows it, three hours on average the book tells me, and now they're glimpsing, flash of her rump going through a gap, skyline cut of her, freckened track of her, and soon they're smellin' her smellin' *her* under the aniseed, her trail's a mile wide this minute, and now look at them, the Lord and Captain Buck and Major Blade, now they're lifting the croobs, now they're flying, now whose tongue's hanging out?, listen to the beagles, where's the fresh young slip?, lying low by the river is the fresh young slip, listen to your beagles *Two to one the Captain evens the Major* they're neck and neck in the straight, where's the fresh young slip?, she's in there hooped in the stink and the sweat and she's all thump-a-thump *Come on the Captain Tight lines Major* . . . The Captain's down! he's down, the Major's away, wins pullin' up, not pullin' up either, he's ploughin' through the scrub, wait, wait, Major gone to ground, ne'er a sound ne'er a sound *Ate up Major stop lickin' your chops* and all join in now please and thank-you, we're a musical nation, a-a-a-a-nd *The Boys who Beat the Black and Tans was the Boys from the County Cork*!

The Windy Tree

—How did that fairytale finish, Herod, do you remember?
—The king's son came up — with the ring, of course — and made shore. He put the ring on a rock, and set about drying himself. And a snake swallowed the ring. And decamped. And that's how it finished.

—I love courage in a gambler, sir, and I see courage in your eye, you're a gambling man and you're far from home, am I right or am I wrong, Mrs Mulligan, you're right ma'am says she. Find the Lady, sir, pastime old as the hills and fresh as dung, some say you'd want to be as quick as catching fleas by candlelight but, sir, in reality it's simple as the sun going down. You'll try your luck, sir, now sir, one two three and the deck guaranteed as the jib remarked to the mainsail, and where, sir, would you say, lies the Lady? . . . *He has a knack!* Right, sir, you'll try a second time, you'll have a bash, your mother won't know and I won't tell her, and one, and two, and three, and now, sir, where, sir, would you say, lies the Lady? . . . *He has a gift!* Lucky number three sang the waves of the sea, never leave it said, sir, your father pupped a bad one, and one, and two, and three, and now, sir, where, sir, would you say, lies the Lady? . . . *His hand is gold!* You'll go far, sir, if you're not hobbled, and if you don't meet rain on the road. And I'll be with you — because I know you — from the cards, sir, it's all in the cards, all far and yonder newses of the follies and the failings of a man . . . Oh, the maid she went to the well to wash, Lillumwham Lillumwhey, the maid she went to the well to wash, dew fell off her lily-white arse, Legaderry, Megaderry, Mett, Mirr, Whoopee, Whey . . .

—This hand. It signs the documents, I thought, it rules . . . And how clean, how spotlessly clean . . . You lifted it then to silence the crowd — and for the first time, it seemed, I was looking at where we live, your indifferent hand above their indifferent faces . . . I went away to my room.
 —You're the born hammer, aren't you? But — whom are you hammering? Finally? And into what? You have the floor.
 —Listen to me. I've been shown the other flame, the one that gives back whatever you bring to it, ice if it's ice you bring, the furnace if it's the furnace you bring.

He's finished with me. I with him. Only not quite. The crazy I detest. With good reason. *You're rocking an empty cradle*, Herodias, he informs me. His pupils never dilate, I notice. Woman's hands. She won't speak to me, up to something, always are at that age. That fairytale, yes, I remember hearing it when I was a child. I'm turning into stretch-marks.

Morning. A servant comes as usual bearing food. I embrace the servant courteously. He jerks back, *Your beard's so rough . . . Some like it*, I joke. She happens to be passing as I say that. She blushes.
 Again: I'm alone. She wanders in. She has a bucket of ice. And a bandage-roll. She sits down on the centre of the floor and, complaining of . . . shin-splints, was it?, starts to bandage her ankles with ice, at intervals looking up to question me.
 My hair freshly washed, gleaming as never in life, is down over my eyes but to my surprise I can see quite clearly and the feeling is one of enormous freedom. I should let my hair down? And the eyes not seen but seeing. A primitive invisibility.

—I had a poet in the other day. Rather like you they're all the time, obliquely or directly, going on about destiny. I put the question, perhaps I was thinking of you, *Has every man a destiny?* He answered, *Alas, no, not every man. To have a destiny you must plunge to the bottom and come up with the ring . . . Like in the fairytale?* I asked. *Exactly.*
 —I heard that story when I was a child — a beautiful story.
 —We all heard it. And my question for you, laddie, is, have you plunged to the bottom, and have you come up with the ring?

Because if not, you haven't the track of a destiny.
 —If I hadn't plunged would I be here?
 —But to the bottom?
 —Not yet — but soon.
 —Can you be so sure?
 —I'm the one plunging.
 —Of course . . . And will you get stuck down there? Or will you come up — with the ring — do you fancy?
 —Bride to the bridegroom, I'm told.

Currently she's never to be seen without this bucket, a perfectly banal bucket, empty or containing whatever, don't ask me, but without even trying she with her bucket is an *event*, everything she touches she animates, in a year or two, a month or two?, less?, her progress will be chain-detonation, I heard her the other day summoning or banishing one of her peers, is that the word, airily, *Don't call me — you've been called*, clever I thought, caught the centre of her, wouldn't you agree, *Don't call me — you've been called* . . .

—High hill or small room? I say that from high hills you can touch the sky. I say that in small rooms two's company. And I say that red wood needs red meat.

I hung I hung on the windy tree
on the tree that none may know
on the tree that none may ever know
what root beneath it runs . . .

In the atrium the young one danced, breathing from the diaphragm, clear eyes measuring the top of the tide.

Deer Crossing

—Sire?
—Fantasy.
—'The rat who came to dinner'?
—Is this gloom?
—Fantasy, Sire, knows no gloom.
—Who told you that?
—She who taught me to suck eggs.
—Clever as a clock, the jester warmed up with a hop-skip-and-jump. And took off.
—At precisely six, three evenings running, the rat came, dined, and left. The couple — happiness at risk — now took action. They fed the cat up to the whiskers — and the cat, comprehending, waited. Next evening, the rat came, there was a struggle, the cat retreated to a corner. The rat ate well, and left. Later, the cat left, and returned next day accompanied by the biggest cat you've ever seen, Sire.

Mark's right eye expanded coldly. The jester gave off sweet flavours of risk.

—The two cats were fed — up to the knob of the skull. And they waited. The rat arrived at six. They fought, Sire, for three days in the kitchen, three days in the yard, and three days on the shore. Nothing was left of the rat. The cats tidied up, strolled off arm-in-arm, and were never, Sire, seen again.

Mark's eyes were on the forest. The jester strolled, declaiming with airy intent.

—Some people ask, *What happened the couple?* And others, *What does it mean?*

Mark gone away, it seemed.

—Did you listen, Sire, to my tale?
—Every word.
—And, Sire?
—What happened the couple?
—*What happened the couple?*
Froth of mirth across unconscionable outrage.
—Yes.
—Quotidian bliss, Sire, decades, at the usual rates.
Wicked now. Consenting adults. And wicked.
—And what does it mean?
—*What does it mean?*
—Yes, the meaning —
—None, Sire.
—None — at all?
—Sire, if you insist —
—I do.
Pause.
—Behold a bubble, Sire, with claws — no harm to it unless encountered by dusk.
—And if encountered by dusk?
—Better it should happen to one than two. And better to two than three.
Mark's eyes drank of the forest.

—When Iseult and I sailed from Ireland we each had a garment specially chosen and laid apart from the rest — two shifts white as snow. That was a hot voyage. Iseult took to wearing her shift all the time — in that heat she couldn't bear anything else on her body. Naturally, it became soiled from constant use — while mine, unused, remained spotless. We arrived here, Iseult married the king, and was about to go to bed with him. Her shift was not as she would have wished it to be. I gave her mine. Unless she's now annoyed with me for that, I don't know how else I may have upset her.
That was what Brangwen said when the two men drew weapons to kill her.
—Tell her what I've said, and that I love her, she added.
The men relented. They tied Brangwen high in a tree (as protection against wolves), cut out the tongue of one of their dogs, and returned to Iseult.

—Her tongue, Madame.
Curl of pink on the broad palm: Iseult looked up from it.
—What did she say?
—That when you and she sailed from Ireland you each had a garment apart — two spotlessly white shifts. The voyage was hot. You took to wearing your shift all the time, you couldn't — such was the heat — bear anything else on your body. You arrived here, married the king, and were about to go to bed with him. Your shift — from constant use on the voyage — was not as you would have wished it to be. Brangwen gave you hers, it had remained unused, it was spotlessly clean.
—And you've killed her?
—As you ordered, Madame.
—The two of you will hang.
—You ordered her killed, Madame.
—I sent her with you to fetch herbs for my headache.
—You ordered her killed, Madame.
—You'll both hang.
—She lives, Madame.
—She lives?
—Lives, Madame.
—Bring her here.
—Iseult, you strange person.
When Brangwen was brought back from the forest, Iseult kissed and embraced her over and over. That storm passed. Brangwen stepped back.
—Iseult, you strange person . . .
Iseult gave herself to the open window, the beech in the garden, the wind's touch light on it, resonant whisper of the foliage running from rim to rim and off into the air.

—Going, going, going, yet never moves at all, Tristan?
—The road.
—Climbs the rock, Tristan, no feet, no bones, no drop of blood?
—The mist.
—Clear sky, Tristan, never a cloud?
—Mirror.
—A man that's not a man kills a bird that's not a bird?
Stymied by Mark.

—Two ends in the water, Tristan, its middle dry?
—Bridge.
—Through the sea without drowning, through the fire without burning?
—Sunlight.
—Greasy strap, Tristan, under the ground?
—Snake.
—Old as the mountains, Tristan?
—The valleys between.
—A man that's not a man kills a bird that's not a bird with a stone that's not a stone?
Stymied.
—White white lady, Tristan, fire on her head?
—Candle.
—Breast but no nipple, Tristan?
—Egg.
—Cuts, cuts, sheds no blood, Tristan?
—Boat before the wind.
—Everyone doing it at the same time, Tristan?
—Growing old.
—A man that's not a man kills a bird that's not a bird with a stone that's not a stone in a tree that's not a tree?
Stymied but lashed back.
—Often seen where it isn't?
Mark stared.
—Often seen where it isn't?
Stared.
—*Blame, blame, blame.*

They remembered that long after but remembered more his replies that first day when someone or other not so innocently asked —
—And what do you do in your spare time, Tristan?
—I ramble the woods.
—What do you do in the woods?
—I count the trees.
—How many trees in the wood, Tristan?
—Two.
—Name them.
—The green. And the withered.

In the seductive voice he kept polished for any or all occasions.
—Two, says he, the green. And the withered.

The Mankeeper

They were cutting the hay this day. He was pleased — he was generally pleased — and a little drowsy from the heat. He lay down to rest on the fresh grass, leaving the men to it, and dozed off. When he awoke the day was far gone and there was no one in the field but himself.

He rose and made his way home to dinner feeling a little out of sorts: the sleep hadn't refreshed him at all. In the house he decided against having dinner.

—You don't feel well? the daughter asked.

—I don't feel right, he said, I feel like the bed, and that's where I'm going.

—You were working too hard, you tired yourself.

He explained that he'd had a long sleep in the field.

—You've a bit of a chill from lying on the fresh grass, you'll be fine in the morning.

He took the night's sleep but in the morning he felt worse, and complained of a kind of a backward and forward movement in his stomach. When evening came and there wasn't the least sign of improvement, they sent for the doctor. The doctor came and questioned and examined. He listened at length to the troubled stomach.

—Now, the patient called out, can't you hear the backwards and forwards of it?

The doctor could hear nothing.

—He's imagined the whole thing, he told the wife and daughter. He'll be all right in a few days, I believe, but let me know.

He left a bottle, and departed.

There was no improvement in a few days; the stirring inside

him had gone away — that was all that could be said. The doctor was sent for once more, and came several days running. In the end he confessed himself baffled, said he'd come no more, and refused to take a penny for his services.

The house was in a state. A second doctor was sent for, and a third, and a fourth. They came singly, and they came in a bunch. They flourished long names for the illness, prescribed potions and ointments, and charged a lump of money for their attentions which were to no avail whatever. Quack-doctors followed the doctors, one came striding over every hill: they muttered and made signs and left powders and distillations and didn't forget to charge either. The patient continued to fade. Six months passed: look at him now and all you saw was shadow in a bottle.

Summer came again. The invalid had a habit of sitting by the door a few hours a day in good weather. He was sitting there one day when along came a travelling-woman he knew. They greeted each other, and the travelling-woman couldn't but say what she felt.

—You're a changed man since I saw you last.

—I'm sick, he told her, I'm more than sick, and no cure in the world.

—Doctors?

—They've taken half the farm, and for what?

—Healers?

—Robbers all.

He told her the whole story, how he'd fallen asleep on the fresh grass that day, the upset that followed, all the comings and all the goings.

—Fresh grass?

—Fresh grass.

—Moist maybe?

—No, no.

—A stream close by?

—Yes, a stream close by.

—Can you show me the spot?

—*The spot*. It was the last place he wanted to see. Even as she asked, he remembered that it must be up on a year to the day since he'd risen from sleep and walked away from it. His grave. Must he go with her to point out his grave? He dragged himself to the field. He showed her the exact spot; the hay had just been cut, and the fresh grass shone. The travelling-woman studied closely the various weeds and herbs growing there, and before long stood up with a small juicy-looking herb between her fingers.

—Do you see that?

—I do.

—Wherever you find that herb you won't have far to look for what's bothering you.

—Go on.

—You've swallowed a mankeeper.

The travelling-woman met the wife and daughter and gave them her information and her advice.

—There's only one man can save him and that's the Prince of Coolavin.

—And where's he to be found? the wife asked.

—On the brink of Lough Gara, it's three days from here, no great journey.

A long discussion commenced. The wife and daughter were in favour of making the journey; anything that offered hope must be tried. The invalid was the obstacle: he'd had enough of doctors — and others, he couldn't be cured, he was too weak to travel, let him die in peace. The discussion started over. Finally, the three women convinced him to try it.

The four of them set out the next day, travelling by horse-and-cart, loaded with provisions. They found lodgings the first night and the second night. They took their fill of rest, especially the invalid who required constant care. On the third day they arrived at the house of the Prince of Coolavin, a fine house on the brink of the lake. They found the owner at home and the invalid told his story.

—Fresh grass you slept on?

—Fresh grass it was.

—A stream close by?

—A stream close by, yes.

—You've swallowed a mankeeper.

The Prince was having his dinner — the main course that day was corned beef. He sat the invalid down at the table, put a great helping of the corned beef before him, and commanded him to eat. The invalid thanked him but drew back — he'd eaten nothing in months, he couldn't touch it.

—Eat that if it was to choke you.

Forced to it, he got through a third of the plate.

—Fine, said the Prince, rest yourself for a few hours now.

In the late afternoon the Prince led him out to a field near the house. The three women followed. There was a stream running through the field. The Prince put him lying down on the bank of the stream, face directly over the water, mouth open and very close to the water.

—Whatever happens, said the Prince, don't move.

The invalid nodded.

The Prince withdrew, and joined the women a few yards back.

Nothing happened for quite a while. At the end of an hour, the invalid felt something stirring inside him, first a backwards and a forwards, then making — at a guess — for the spoon of the breast, on in the direction of the throat, next in his mouth, moving out to the tip of the tongue, next no move at all. About a minute later, he felt a stirring in his mouth again, the dart out to the tongue-tip, and this time *plop* with it into the water.

—Don't move, the Prince warned.

The invalid didn't move. In a few minutes he experienced a repeat of the stirrings, first the backwards and the forwards, then making headway, up into the mouth, out to the tip of the tongue, sliding back, no move at all, forward again, and *plop* again into the water. It was a procession after that, a dozen in all.

—There's your clutch, said the Prince, now for the mother.

The invalid was close to exhaustion, and growing fretful. When another hour passed without incident, he made to rise, he could take no more. The Prince and the travelling-woman had to go forward and forcibly hold him down, one to each shoulder: there they stayed. The wife and daughter, pale the pair, watched from their same station.

A short time passed, and the invalid felt a stirring inside that surpassed anything so far, a stirring that was almost a tearing, forcing its way up to the throat, through and into the mouth, and resting there. The invalid moved. His hand shot to his mouth but, if he was quick, the mankeeper was quicker: back down the throat with her, gone.

—Didn't I tell you not to move? snapped the Prince, you've maybe frightened her for good.

But he hadn't. She came up again in about twenty minutes, the same tearing and pushing, up into the mouth, timidly there for a minute or two, scouting, back and forth, back and forth, out at last to the tip of the tongue, and *plop* — seven times the plop of any of the others — into the water.

—Well you knew the tub of butter when you found it, the Prince roared after her.

They carried the invalid back to the house. He said nothing for three days. The first words he said were:

—I'm a new man.

The Harper's Turn

The most beautiful one ever wind or sun played on, and adored the king, her father.

Dance for your Daddy
my little babby
dance for your Daddy
my little lamb

you'll have a fishy
in your little dishy
you'll have a fishy
when his boat comes in —

When he fell on the field, she searched the carnage, found his body, sucked the wounds, drank there, took to the wilds, grew hair, fur, killer-claws, struck as she pleased man and beast, sucked ever and always, sucked the wounds, drank them dry.

 —Rewards galore, the victorious king spread his girth, victims also.
 —So I believe.
 —We prefer to have her brought in alive.
 —Naturally.
 —Not at all 'naturally'. Don't forget she's a ruthless killer. A score have gone after her. You should have seen the bodies.
 —No harper among them?
 —Hunters. Warriors. A few priests.
 —I'll try my luck.

—Have wit, will you? The world's full of bad harpers.
—That's how we know good ones. I leave tomorrow.
—You're mad.

He made for the mountains.
A white stag crossed his path more than once.
—You follow, he addressed the animal eventually, and you lead. That's your portion.
The stag never paused but a nurturing answer pulsed.
And a woman appeared, woman he would have halted: on her forehead a profusion of curls, glossy bald the back of her head.
—Who are you?
—Make a fist in your pocket, she counselled, continue the ritual.
And gone. Bald back of her head melting through trees.
He had thought to grab her by the forelock. And was left to reflect: you know what thought did.
The body, he recalled the riposte of a lover, never lies.
Simply wouldn't be bothered.
In any case, unable.

He pitched his tent on a lonesome slope above the river, settled himself, and began to play. Days passed. The forest around him stilled, a listening quiet. But not her listening. He played on.
He'd been there a week when one morning he heard a different colour, registered her ear live in the foliage.
He didn't lift his head, continued playing, let the music run — for her. And was aware — of her awareness that it was so.
Late afternoon, and, through a scatter of grace-notes, he could tell she'd left. He stopped playing, and lay down to sleep.
She returned with dusk. At any rate, he woke then to find her sitting close by, a strangled stag beside her.
She presented the strangled stag.
He cut the stag's throat, skinned it, quartered it.
He made a fire, put granite stones in it.
He dug a hole, filled it with water.
He wrapped the meat, put it in the hole, fed the stones, cooked the meat.
They ate.
He stood her in the hole where the lukewarm broth and the

melted fat of the stag was and massaged her every part and worked the broth and the oils and the juices over her and into her until sweat broke and ran.

He made a bed for her, he spread the hide of the stag under her and his cloak above her.

A quick learning.
She presented
he cut
he made
he wrapped
fed the stones
he stood her
he rubbed
he spread.
He played. They played.
Fur fell away, claws, all fell away, again before him and all sun and wind the most beautiful.

Once he heard her laughing in her sleep, spoke of it next morning.

—Last night I heard a lovely story — from myself.

They had their spell in the mountains. She saw him day after day pulling a shadow inside him. Sometimes she wanted to wash his feet. That had happened before.

Often and often I had a wish to wash his feet, bathe them, wash them, dry them, he wanted me to, I knew that unspoken, I never did, there's one of my should haves windfall now under the tree.

And his chin with a trick of swerving betimes slightly, as, rue on the smile, to ride some anticipated blow.

—What is it you look for? she enquired.

—Words that will stick in my throat.

She took his hands, kissed his eyes.

—Sometimes I feel you're watching me through harp-strings.

He studied her.

—Once I was with a girl and we saw — imagine the ugliest savage of a dog you can imagine. What breed was it? She went up to ask. Leaning, she patted the dog. At once the dog was gentle, a wonderful shape. The two made a picture. I shrank before it.

—Shrank, did you?

She drew him to her.

The white stag returned, woke him — nudge of a hoof — from deepest slumber.
—You came here with nothing, the stag said, now give it back.
—How?
He looked up into the indomitable eyes.
—Now give it back.
Those fading hoof-taps haunted the slope.
And the woman returned, stopped him on his way to wash in the river.
—Good-morning.
—And to you.
Her curls shone.
—Listen to me.
—I'm listening.
—The world's full of bad harpers.
Bald back of her head. Winking good-bye.

—Let me bathe you, she requested.
—All right.
She killed a stag, prepared it, cooked it, and they ate. Then she stood him in the hole where the lukewarm broth and the melted fat of the stag was and massaged his every part and worked the broth and the oils and the juices over and into him until sweat broke and ran.
She made a bed, spread the hide of the stag under them, and his cloak above.
And knew as she lay beside him that, were she to bathe him thus a hundred times, the question was other.
She could hear noises inside him, the forest attentive.
—What are you thinking? she ventured.
—The way that river digs.
—And what else?
—The gape of the ford.
Silence a while.
—There's a shadow you won't touch, she said.
—True.
—Why not?
—My idleness to stalk it a while yet.
As they were dropping to sleep, he offered:
—I love like a spectator, my love.

He was hooked on a story, one look told you that. What was it? It had to do with his father — or was it his grandfather? — and it went like this: *Spills of light teemed in the crevices of a stone wall. The old man drifted along the face of the wall. His hand rose, slipped between blue stones, searched, withdrew, over and over. There wasn't a sound. The wall swallowed the drifting hand, held, released it. The spills of light warmed the hand, touched the old man as he moved along.*

That picture was the music he played. And you listened.

Their mountain spell was ending.

—I'd never kill another hare, he swore, finishing an account of some hunt he'd been on.

And she realised — it sang in the phrase — that he was a hare who played the harp and knew skills of healing and carried a wound from the shore.

—When people ask me, he also told her, what kind of life is it being a harper, I tell them: I'd recommend it to all my children.

Chin swerving slightly, as, rue on the smile, to ride some anticipated blow.

Gravely she walked beside him. They were expected — a large crowd had gathered, swelled at their approach.

—We're celebrities, he joked.

She said nothing, measuring this climate of no surprise, everything known, it appeared, everything arranged.

—You're welcome.

They took him away.

—Why are you taking him away?

—For questioning.

The king examined her with interest.

She looked at the ground.

—Speak to us, won't you?

Her brown foot played the grass. She watched it part the lush stems, bare fraught roots. She stood there. She listened. Her whole head listened and heard.

Cliodhna's Wave

One towards whom the men came with stones in their sleeves. One who made, as directed, for the shore, and saw the currach appear, high in the bow and with a stern of copper, two young men aboard, each one robed shoulder to heel.
—Will you take me?
—If you're quite alone.
One who stepped into the spray and sprang aboard and was taken away.

The green severities of the sea. Matters at the worst, a rider on a pale-grey horse rose out of the heave and whip, horse and rider dry as the floor of the oven. They must bow. They bowed. He lifted them on to the horse, nudged the reins.
—It's always desirable to have two notions, the voice so level commended, one to demolish the other.
The currach turned on its side, followed them across the waves.

—What about that bird?
On a high sill a bird with beak of iron and tail of fire. It rattled plumage. Everywhere weapons fell. Those who picked them up stiffened on the spot, stuck there. The rod of copper — taken from the currach was handy. He raised it, cut the air. The bird fell.
—What remains then but to go to her?
—Who are you?
—Just one thing: speak to her from the ends of your bones.
The tall one moved off, water slopping from the thigh-high boots.
—I'm Sweet-One-Day and Sour-the-Next.

The fiddler plying his bow across a shank of bone that shone white and cast a red shadow.
—I'm three by three, the fiddler cried, Crooked against Crooked, Corner against Corner, and Trick against Treachery.
And:
—If I promised to bring it *to* you, I did not promise to bring it *for* you.

So they met.
Her smooth side to him.
His smooth side to her.
—Mine at the ebb and mine at flood tide.
—Yours at the ebb and yours at flood tide.

Before they left, there was that gift of a cup, green and shapely.
—This will tell you what to drink.
Cliodhna observed the play.
—Where was it made?
—A whale that was washed ashore here. When we cut him up we found that in the heart. So we call it *The Product of the Beast*.
That straightened your eyes all right.

The morning shone on them.
—You've dolphin hands.
—Listen to me—
—But I hear . . .
Their kisses turned to birds.
The Boyne beckoned. They were bound for the Palace of the God of Love. From the heaps of the deeps the eels whistled fair wind and good tide. Ireland came into view. The land breeze. Smoke, clay, blossom. Waterford, Wexford, Wicklow, hills playing with the sea. The leak in his heart gaped. He lulled her to sleep. He turned the currach. Sole of the oar and palm of the oar. He rounded Ireland south-about and kept going until he came to the harbour of Glandore. He'd land here and find food. He moored the currach, looked at her sleeping, kissed bright hair that stirred to the breeze.
—You've taken away the look of my life.
Whisper, and he slipped ashore. As he stepped into the forest he heard the howl of the wave.

Cliodhna . . .
A branch cut him across the eyes.
—Lick lips for your supper.

   Also one who loved animals. When he died his cattle gathered about his body. They nosed, they tugged, they poked. With their horns they tore him to pieces, stampeded a province, and, reaching the Boyne, paused to slake thirst, to taste of Boann the Beautiful, that Boann who dared the burdened pool, drew from it three volumes of water — at the cost of an eye, an arm, and a thigh, faced seaward, and — the waters eager and at one — seaward was borne.

The Hospital Barber

The magic cow — sieve there instead of bucket — gave until she bled, cut loose, tore a gap in the rim of the valley, and vanished into the sea near Howth.

   —Get it out of there — if only for cosmetic reasons.
(Cosmetic, mind you.)
   —It's your cyst, all the same to me.
   —Damage likely?
   —No.
   —What's your advice?
   —Your cyst.
The hospital barber: *Christ, you're a hairy man.*
   —Why?
   —Just pop up. Live a thousand years you mightn't get another on that spot.
   —Take it out.
Done. And, lo and behold, another pops up on the same one, two new ones for more than good measure on the left, epidydimal harvest, *sub rosa*.
   —Feel lighter now?
   —Oh considerably.

Heavy traffic, thunder and lightning, holding that child in his arms, sheltering, a good feeling and a bad, mind the child, mind the child, ever walk a cobbled yard a wine-glass tied to your ankle, the child a fragile old dog for the hard road had been pulled out of ditches, quagmires, marl-holes and midden-humps, indestructible, breath, clay, open hand, and telegram-boy — *Frog needs no hammer in the rainy season . . .*

A land dispute, yet another, warning letters by the dozen, and the father had a dream, no, met a ghost while walking the road: the dog refused to pass the gate of the broad field, stood there trembling, and the father knew, leaned over the gate, looked right under the hedge, an old man sitting there, stranger, wearing plain as plain — the father recognised it at once — the hat of the grandfather long dead and gone — *Mind your own business.* On the Monday, as previously announced, Mark entered the field, commenced to plough, and the sniper, all for symmetry, allowed him three furrows, then — British Army trained — shot the horses, first the white, next the grey, next Mark through the forehead, they heard the shots, the father found him, neighbours refused water, their need greater than his.

—You sound tense?
She admires herself before like Diane de Poitiers — some Actaeon gallivanting to his noon appointment, skin 'em and ate 'em, a wise animal, a shore creature, but why keep knocking glasses, breaking mirrors?
—You steal all my best stories, she snapped.

In that land the old were young and the young old, the old one banged whatever was handy with whatever was handy and shouted — When I was young, when I was young . . . I was in my alley then . . .

Dawn-light or thereabouts (this child takes minding) and a garden, sliding away from the garden a woman and her daughter, the garden pool, a dog surfacing, friend, pointer, swims clear, white and brown, and is the child who strolls where wild orchids, winnowed blue, lacemaker texture, grow: among them, turn of the hand, breath, he gathers pollen, pollen, pollen, ambles on.

Left of the Door

Take the can, a stiff arm, take the can, fixing eyes high on walls, on doors. Creak of the can, your steps, rattle-and-click of the outer door. Step outside, sour May cold, slap of the wind, and stand stiff as a board. The spade left of the door. Eyes fixed, keeping the eyes at eye-level, reach, and gather the spade with the left hand, and turn, and past the kitchen window, dragging open the small gate, crossing the lane, and stepping on to the dung-heap. And advancing to the middle of the dung-heap, stand.
 Looking away, leave down the can on a level spot. Do it quick. Grip the spade, and scrabble on the face of the dung-heap, root and scoop and hoke a spot, claw and tear. Drop the spade. Looking away, turn to the can. And take the can, and looking away, not looking away, spill it there, scorch of poor pink-flesh in the shit and the mess. Down the can, and grab the spade, and over it, cover it, maul and root dung back there, cover it, put more, that'll do, more, that'll do, leave it.
 Take the can, spade and the can, turn away, stand up, lift your head, and fix on the sea, the stretch of it, the sea this day, rag where your chest was, and slap of the wind.

 Step up on the dung-heap, and move to the middle. And stand and listen to yourself. Leave down the can on a level spot. Sprout looking up at you. Take the spade, and go to it, shoulder to the wind. Scoop, don't rush this, clear a basin in the dung-heap, give it shape, take time, you have time, your back a hard curve, face blind as the spade. Take your time. Leave down the spade. Turn to the can. Take the can, and care over what you're about, and watching, spill all into the basin, and look, and meet the whole slither and slop, blood and the mess and morsel raw on the dung. Turn away, and take the spade, and fill the basin, root on the cover of dung, and root more, and secure it, and then some more, and leave it now.

Lean on the spade, and fix on the stretch of sea.

Take the spade, and to it as they taught you, wield the spade, find a spot on the heap that will take the cut of the spade, moisture patch, and give it a rhythm, and make the small grave, know what you're about, good foot down and a foot by a foot, up on that, tidy it there, that'll do. Leave aside the spade. Go to the can. Stoop over it, and put in your hands. And lift out the sliver, slippery, and no weight, no weight at all, filmy man-woman of ours. Take it, dripping, and place in the one foot by one, set it there, scrap of her, lost bit. Go back to the can, and take the can, and again to the spot, and spill it all in. The dung drinks. The can aside. Pick up the spade. And fill with care, using the spade as they taught you, finding the beat of it, letting the cut of the wind take your bones. Fill it, and fill it, and tend it, and more, and leave the spade aside. And down, and by the small heap, and cry what you have.

The can and the spade. Walk straight, child. Spade to the left of the door. Inside, the quiet, love, and the fire low.

Thalassa

First he planted too much. Next he delayed reaping. The men were to come Saturday. They arrived Monday. Nothing was ready. Not even water in the house.
 —Bring a bucket of water from the stream, the maid told him.
 He put the bucket in the stream and watched it fill. He heard the sea, and he looked. It was coming towards him. He saw a boat, an old man in the boat, red-haired, and whirling three yellow balls. The boat came right up to him, kicked his knees. He lashed back. At once: into the boat and away.

 The landing was rough, the shore rougher. A man in the guise of a woman? A woman astray? His movements rang ungainly. A light, a house, the youngster within sometimes a boy, sometimes a girl, dressing for a wake.
 —Will you come?
 —Sure.
 The wake was for a woman dead in child-birth. During the night the child began to cry. One of the women took it out of the cradle. There was no soothing it. The child was being handed from one woman to another.
 —Give it to the strange woman.
 This was done. The child slept like a thrush.
 White light of day:
 —The child's yours to mind.
 That was seven years' work.

 A house in the middle of a bog. Rumpus inside. Two cradles, one each side of the fire, an old woman lying in each, a rope of straw between the cradles, the pair rocking each other, and singing

> *The Kingstown people dressed in black*
> *Pickin' winkles and cartin' wrack*

    The shore. Slack of the tide and flat calm. A house in the mouth of the waves. By the door an old woman laying into a dish of sea-cabbage. She looked up. Bluest eyes ever seen and nose to draw blood from the wind.
    —What weakens men? Corn warm from the kiln.
    She dug into the sea-cabbage again, finished it.
    —The red sea is coming from the east, and the torrent is coming from the west.
    She licked the dish, flung it over her shoulder, pointed to the headland.
    A woman was walking straight-backed out to the very tip of it, web of bawneen on her shoulders. She began to unwind it slowly. As the web unwound it floated out and down towards the house. It whipped and snapped as if the evening was blowing a gale. The old woman lifted a hand, the web was called back, woman and web spun from his sight like a thread of the mist.

Ghost Children

The cinema gloaming. What's she searching for?
—Put that back on for me?
—Sure. Pierced?
—Yes . . .
Gently. Glaze of unknowing across the fingertips, the lobe.
—That okay?
—Grand. Thanks.
And afterwards:
—Thanks. That was grand.
—It was . . .
—And the meal too —
—You're a growing girl.
—Well, see you soon —
—Sure . . .
Peck-peck.
—'Bye.
—'Bye.
Master of the graceless farewell, I watch a daughter melt back into her life.

The Zoo —
The theatre —
The cinema —
The Museum —
The Castle —
Christ Church —
St Patrick's —
The National Gallery —

The Municipal —
The Young Scientists' Exhibition —
Sandymount Strand —
The Phoenix Park —
St Michan's — God preserve us —
The Zoo —
Spare us the Zoo. Another dose of the Zoo and we'll strangle the giraffe.

Well, for a long time, forever — tell the truth, on your infrequent visits to the city, their city now more than yours, you'd see a head, hint of profile, the colour of hair exactly right, adjacent details right or eerily approximate, and — the compass spitting — decide, *That must be him or her*, one of them, some of them, the conviction total and fragile, here goes, and twist direction, and follow, shunt through the traffic, gather speed and find an angle, by now assured — and palpitating. And look. And go back then to your quiet. You've had your gallop for today. Your thumpety-thump-thump . . .

—Where are you living now?
—Who's living with you?
—What's that strange ring you're wearing?
—Whose is that hair on your lapel?
—What's that look in your eye?
—What's your name? Butter-an'-crame?

Photographs the worst, one in particular, on the sideboard of your brother the priest, apostle of duty, and more. Colour-photo. There they are, smiling and dazed a bit, the world coming in lumps against the bric-à-brac frame of the shot. Semi-orphaned, they look out at you and past you in accusation alluringly mild.

Muddy November field. Take them for a walk and tell them. Get off the road to tell them. So you all blunder into this muddy field. And you father your announcement. They drift about you there. We whimper and stutter under a whey sky. And later down the road on your own, the dog — scattered as the hour that was in it — padding behind.

Once upon a time one of them, the youngest, said, an arrange-

ment at issue for the month after next, Easter or Whit or —
—Oh, I never look at calendars.
Another time one said:
—Wish I had you for a teacher.
And once, this was kicking a ball around in the Phoenix Park, one of them tackled you like the wind flinging open a door and the two of you fell wrestling on the bouncy summer grass.

Across a table from you the growing boy. Napery dotted with checkpoints. Cutlery and delph neutral to recalcitrant.
—I wanted to be able — when you grew up — to look you in the eye, that's all.
Lifts his head. Looks you in the eye. Splits your eye open. Desists.

—You'll find, of course, as they grow older —
—Thanks.
—You know that.
—I do. And I don't.
—Why don't you have a good scream?
—Frighten myself?

College Park, an October afternoon. Lemon-yellow the leaves, tickle of frost, fervent sun. The match desultory. We watch, half-watch. The poise of this day. Simple as love. Where've they gone? Look at them. Remnants of a wooden barrier become their tumble-down stile. They perch. Compact. Breathe themselves.
Be still.
Seasons folding us, I name my hostages to fortune.

Pot Black

The most beautiful thing ever said to me a woman said.
—Let's make love, I suggested.
—I don't make love, I just fuck.
—All right — let's just fuck.
—No — with you I couldn't just fuck, I'd have to make love.
And another said to me once, it came out in a rush as sometimes happens.
—You know sometimes I think I could go to the end of the world with you except I feel all you're looking for is a reflection.
—A reflection?
—Yes.
—Aren't we all mirrors, after a fashion?
—You're cracked.
—But not broken.
—Wait for it.
—I crave it. Be a brick. Deliver yourself.
But she would not.
And the worst thing ever said to me a woman said.
—You're not in your body any more, your white body, and it's never been loved.

She spoke from such high surety. The thought scrubbed my bones, *This one wants to kill me*. I had to say something. So I sang of — what else? — survival play and double-play, stratagems of the night and bucklers of the heart. I opened to her my book of device and distraction — that cornucopia of the fecund, I spoke of and performed — *and performed* — my entire repertoire of dances: recreational, constitutional, native, imported, callipyginous, gauche, *danse ersatz, danse verité*, and *danse macabre*, my tempered evangelical and my uncontrollable blast, I said — You, ma belle, you're talking to a transformer of sorrow, *ennui*, and the glare horizon, haven't you heard of *Eternal mind's eternal recreation? Transformation, transformation, and again transformation!*

She was looking at me as if I were the mother and father of all voodoo, I who tended the bubbling stew of the swamps infernal, but my cadenced tirade knew only impetus, impetus — Join me, I said, join me in the dervish pentathlon outlined above — all right, adumbrated — and who's to say you and I, looped, might not spin past the fear of danger to encounter the danger of fear?

—You're just moving the furniture about.

That's what the woman said.

Alex Higgins, *l'admirable* Alex, told me four things in our brief conversation. Never forgotten them, don't believe I ever will. *The nap of the cloth varies from hour to hour* — it's poetry, isn't it, when you think about it, pure poetry. *Take full advantage of any opening.* Finally, *Grow the killer touch.* 'Grow' — mind you. The killer touch.

The Irish, the Poles, twin tribes, and look out: potato-eaters, spirit-drinkers, and, of course — from their respective northern skies — the furious sense of grievance. Dad: preacher hands, face of a troll.

—We've root-crop hearts.

—What d'ye mean, Dad?

—We're enraged quadrupeds, man. Eat or be eaten.

Mom? Baltic pewter the prehensile eye. On the sunniest summer day the sense of a skiing holiday crystalline beside her. Had a theory about *content*. Content? *The communication of what is secret by what is secret.* Naturally she fell taciturn. One day silent. Last words — *I wish to be assumed.* No — *desolé* — last words, addressed to me, conversation, actually.

—What are you doing?

—Considering.

—You'll die considering.

And gone.

But I don't wish to leave wrong impressions — of either. Mom — for example, early days. A noise, inaudible, she was always

listening to — or for.
—What is it, Mom?
—Low *doh* of arrival, high *doh* of departure.
And Dad, near the end.
—Never, son, be in any place where they are not on your side.
Delivered *con moto*.
—They?
Smiled. Expired.

L'admirable Alex at the start of our brief meeting, Alex at the top, best in the world.
—How do you do it, Alex?
—It's all an illusion.
—Don't say that, Alex, don't — *please*.
—It's an illusion, a grand illusion.
He was laughing — but in dead earnest.

She had lazy lips — that she never underestimated. She gave me fingertips. I had hands, fingers. She arrived. I had fingertips.
—There's a water-drop in every fingertip. Touch me with those.
Afterwards, a good while later, being in the locality, I went to stare the house. Up the path. I must see — a particular room. Looked in. Harvest of emptiness. Known furniture, familiar objects — lamp, breadbin, spicerack plus — *O taste and see* — the emptiness. I stood there. I left.
They say that on a certain floor of the building you always love the one once loved — that floor being the hardest to find. To this bejayzus credo I do now give assent. So help me Christ.
The night you left — the night of the morning you left — I went to bend myself towards sleep in that bed which had been our miscreant and prodigious playground. On the pillow, sheets, smell of your body, limbs. That was the dear breath. Still — worth it. I do believe. A head-on meeting. Tangential also.
—A woman's body remembers, she'd say, but the cock forgets. It crows thrice and it forgets.
Anthem of hers. Right. And wrong. Right, *A woman's body remembers*. Wrong, *The cock forgets*. The cock remembers, the cock remembers. And the cock forgets.

These (summarising) pointers from Alex, I play them over daily, proffer them to all my children —
—*Use* the cue — it's not a head of lettuce.
—*Spin* — like everything else — gradually evaporates.
—Imagine it's pitch dark. *Now:* hit it where it shines.

Foggy Hair and Green Eyes

Foggy hair and green eyes, a friend female, close to the action, took the liberty of describing her that way. I like the description. Love it, even. Women describing women always command my unqualified attention. *Foggy hair and green eyes*... I don't know what — or I half-know, three-quarters doubt I know — what was going on between us. The *via negativa*, and yet not quite. The sea was up, of that there's no doubt, and — at times — I'd go so far as to say there was white water swirling close. And yet. I was hooked, after a fashion. She could, it's true, be stolidly humourless. I told her a story once in which a rat came to a bad end, a bad and a bloody. 'Discrimination against the rat', she commented — and no more. But I forgave her that. I had no alternative.

My recollection is that I didn't get the address from her — that would have been far too open. I got the name of the street from her, and the number of the house from some directory or other. That took several days, could have been drugged weeks, even, the dilatory beat was important. Perhaps I'd glimpsed her a few times — and there'd been our usual circling exchanges. Or perhaps no glimpse of her at all, the trigger there. Or perhaps a few 'phone calls — she had rights to a communal 'phone distinguished for its unpaid bills and consequent raffish uncertainty. I believe that was it, in fact. No reply. Or she's out. Or line engaged for days. All right, *Start walking*.

I knew the general direction. Down the main street, towards the idle railway-station, and away to the left. Edge of the town. It was Fall. But I can't pretend leaves for the burning and pastel hues. Yet the Fall — all right, *Autumn* (but Fall for me) — everywhere. Pendant. And right for this expedition. And not mattering at all. The central awareness was the within-weather, rub-a-dub of fever at the yielding, at the incorrigible here-we-go-again. The body floated between hot and cold. Bold-sweat. This was the old familiar bold-sweat owning the pores, the blood even more. You're a hunter, she said once. Are you? Listen. Bones barking?

    I hit the street. A straggling street. I rejoiced in that, and the deduction from the numbers that the house was hundreds of yards off, quite close probably to where the street became a dirt-track and sloped off into fields and meagre woodland. On the street. Dead of afternoon, that hour pointedly chosen. Avoid the traffic of lunch-time, and the five o'clock shift. Find an empty hour within reach of dusk. Say your prayers. Hum your wares. Radiate. What? Health — good clean corpuscles, pert for nones, choiring *a cappella* and the cat lappin' soup in the corner.

    No sin of idleness on this street. School-children and the occasional flurry of bike-races, theirs, and dogs in combat on the borders of that. Madame hoovering the car. Grand-dad staring the roses. Ripe distractions. Normality. Only birdsong needed. My kingdom, my kingdom for a linnet. No matter. A woman window-cleaning. Nothing wrong with that. Rococo weather-vane on the *qui vive*. You're empty. And brimming, aren't you? A thing, proceeding, in the reliable noise-level of the reliable street until, happily, coming towards the house, quiet. The light — poised. The breath — drifty. Would she be there? Most unlikely, at this hour. But — she might. Or she might coast out of the afternoon behind him. Or. He tried to look plain. Someone looking for a house. The house. Of a friend.

    It stood quite on its own. The street was disintegrating out here. On its own: that's to say you could circle it — if you dared — from a distance of twenty yards or more. And pretend, with some hope of success, that you had no tie whatever to the place. Walk past it first. Get the value of that, just walking past her house. No lights on. There were stray lights in some of the houses around, the dusk wasn't laggard in these parts. Bless the incipient dusk, it soothed, it muffled, let it play there. Meanwhile, walk well past the house, a man going for a late afternoon stroll, eyes on the smudges of timber ahead. Was the house empty? Seven or eight rooms in it, you'd estimate. Well, the lights — or lack of them — should give a pretty clear indication. And there were other tests that might be applied.

He turned. And back slowly towards the house. There was a light, he could see now, in the kitchen area. Had that been on? Did it signify? A sure bet they left lights on all over the place. There was, all the same, a distinction to be made. A light simply left on; a light that had a person close to it, the person not necessarily visible but the vibrations spelling a presence. No other lights, anyway, besides that kitchen one. He felt — weightless. With mischief. More than mischief. He felt tainted.

The start of circling the house. Not a precise circle, of course, sweetly wavering. The ground undulant, better again. The waves. A first for you? Yes. I'd stood on the footpath, stared windows, this city or town or that country road, but circling the house, eyes pinned on the house, scrutinising, that was a first. It yielded nothing except the toxic pulse of its own dithering progress, if progress it was. And yes, it was. Because it led to a next move, and quickly. You can't foosther over circling a house, no one will contradict that. You draw the circle, you taste what can I see, am I being observed, you measure the weight of activity inside, and, the fill of your stare of windows under your belt, you desist. That's done.

Now the door. How open of you. Striding, not striding, sidling up to the porch. *Stoop*, they call it. Your feet on the clamorous wooden steps. *So here you are, you're welcome, stranger.* There was a screen-door, hooked back. The door itself was inches ajar. I see. Through the glass top half of the door, the hallway. Nondescript. But not for me. The light in the kitchen seemed far away. Not a sound in the place. He stood there. Would someone come running down that stairs? Some door — hers? — spin open? No, nothing. You have such an appetite. Unappeasable. Really.

He rang the bell, knowing it wouldn't work. The button had that pallor. Or he knew he would be encouraged to knock, let that sound loose. How long had he been here? The bell didn't work. There was such a lure in that door just a bit open. Encourage me. If someone appeared he'd enquire — straining for the negligent, and be told — *No, she's out, care to leave a message?* No, I'll try again, thanks. And slink into retreat. So pray no one would appear. Unless, impossibly, she. But better no one. Especially not she. You want her to see you in this situation? Standing on the step perilous? The late afternoon was dangerously, agreeably, still. Knock.

He knocked. Boldly. He listened. No stir. No one in the kitchen? He glanced up and down the street. All quiet. No one watching him, questioning his intrusion. Presence. Not yet intrusion. Knock again. And he did. Healthy, healthy. There was no one there. No one in the house. The place was all his. He'd come this far, and he was in luck. And now your breath had an edge. Deckled. Push open the door. And float inside. And stand in the nondescript hall. There's the blackguard 'phone. A few newspapers. Caps and coats, left-behinds, on a raddled hall-stand. Protect yourself. Quickly. You have entered a house.

—Anybody home?

It rang through the house. Not rang. Hung hollow on the landing above. And was gone.

—Anybody home?

So the place was definitely empty. He closed the door behind him, not quite closed, left less ajar than he'd found it, closed it as much as he dared. *Oh safety* . . . The kitchen. Steps unhesitating, noisy even, establish the high honourable intent of all this, stride towards the light. Empty kitchen. Dishevelled sink. A calendar hanging awry, the wrong month looking at the world. Harmless zone of the kitchen. Leave it to heaven. Back up the hall, listening, keeping an eye. And what *will* you say if someone finds you roaming this house? *Du calme, du calme*. It was good to stop and listen to the stillness. And sip the next motion.

He switched on a light in the hall. Not a necessity but a tactical consideration. The stabiliser of the quotidian, if you don't mind. Well, you're here, and now what? That what was plain — but would it be granted? Let it be granted. You deserve it. Don't you think? Rooms along the hall. Rooms above. But those along the hall (he wasn't an upstairs burglar, that wasn't in him — yet) were the ones that mattered. Two. One door, shut, that one beside him. The other, nearer the front door, slightly ajar. He knocked on the door beside him, the knock — peremptory and polite — that we reserve for the room we know to be empty. He opened the door. Glanced in. Bedroom-cum-study — as, no doubt, all the rooms were — but not in use. Waiting for whoever. Disconsolate mattress. On the desk an impeccably even farewell of dust. One book on a shelf of sorts. Cheap dictionary. Shut the door.

All right. Along the hall, and, staying on pulsing alert, to the next door. And wait a moment. To gather caution — which came and went without much control. What do you want of her anyway? She of you? Speaking for myself, everything, I want everything. Within limits. Naturally. You want to move from the circling to the touching. You want to see how the touching might touch you both. How clear-sighted the ambition. Leave this house before you're caught. Caught? Yes. He looked at the front door. Thought of departure. See it through when you're this far. Anyway, as for leaving, you can't, you couldn't. You're not ready to leave yet. Listen. Nothing. He pushed open the door of the room beside him.

It was her room. That jacket was hers, other bits and pieces he recognised. The bed, undressed, struck him. Her bed. Undressed. Ordinary. High-explosive. On from the bed, you haven't all day. Robe draped across a chair. No, flung there, she never draped anything. Scattered shoes. They held him. Pitched there. This was her room. True to her. A *sometimes* quality to it. *I'm here sometimes.* Was there a hairbrush — or are you making that up? There was a cheap hairbrush. Let there be a hairbrush, hers, lying on the flimsy dressing-table which doubled — fecklessly — for desk. Not the studious type. You never shifted from the doorway. Didn't dare? Yes, you did.

Don't you remember? It's coming back. You dared all right, there was no retreat then, giddy with the scents and shadows of her you entered the room. The word *sumptuary* blazed from every thesaurus you'd ever pawed. A Paris dusk. Christ, that scent of hers . . . And if she were here now . . . She is here . . . This is her room . . . You have been to her room, in her absence, without her knowledge, you have had this phantom taste. You stepped into the room, looked about, that bed, hers, and, such a sliding within you, you left the room. It was that or faint. And you don't hang around in such circumstances, no one will contradict that.

Surely there was a musky temptation, a musk-and-civet ripple, to leave a note, some sign, anyway. A token. A spoor. Your mark, your name and nation. There had to be. Then to imagine that look of puzzlement stirring the foggy hair and green eyes, amusement. Wrath? Hardly. She'd understand. This was, after all, a duet. It was a shooting-match — but neither side had guns. Or both sides had chosen to use blanks. Are there blanks on such expeditions? Rooms, imaginings, scents, scattered shoes — call those 'blanks'? Writers always want to leave a note. That's the trouble with writers. One trouble. Leave a note means — at such an hour — a recipe for over-writing. *Always over-wrote, revised in the morning.* . . She didn't say that. The one observing the action said it. But she would have said it, with closer acquaintance . . . She might say it yet . . . adding her own inimitable and gossamer curlicues . . .

Out. And into the hall. Leave her door ajar, as you found it. You're safe now, and clear, barring accident. To the front door. Leave the hall light on. The front door. And out. And bang it, lightly bang it behind you. It clicks shut. And you're on the porch. And walking away. Weak in the body. Dim in the soul. The noise inside you. The soft pedal thunder, the tundra crackle. Wonder what your eyes look like this minute. *Stop looking at me with the points of your blue eyes.* Are you sweating? No. Or it's cold-sweat. Are you walking the earth? What are you looking for? I don't know. Streets in the air and bridges over the wild red sea . . . Well, you'll find out some day when the ducks have eaten all the dirt.

I stopped a bit down the street. I want to go back to the house, into it, into her room again . . . But you can't. You pulled the door shut, you heard the lock click . . . What a blunder, what an absurdly definitive action in a climate where fog is elixir and mist ambrosia . . . and haze the . . . You shut the door, you heard the lock click, that's that. . . No other way in permissible — for your kind of visit . . . Walk away . . . *Amadhán* to have made such an elementary mistake. Her room, her bed, her shoes, that hairbrush, scent . . . *What are you at? Get out of here.*

He started walking — with impetus. With decision. It felt wonderful. If that was the word. He walked, walked. Wonderful, it felt.

Wing-Beat, Wing-Feather

He was by no means ordinary. All right, you'll say, but who *is* ordinary? I know what you mean — and yet he was special. He was a master of the art, feared by the many, loved by the few. A master of what art? Be patient, that will be revealed.

Also: he was in love. And was loved. She loved him, as he loved her, of that there's no doubt. Watching them together, you could tell instantly, that's the way with love. A light around the body, right? as all know. A light around *their* bodies, lovers, together. The song of the world — or one of the songs.

The event, in any case, illustrates the point fully. Events, I should say. Climactic events — but let us avoid the baroque. It was all quite straightforward. Veritable post-modern ABC. And D. *D minus* — she'd be inclined to say — but she wasn't a whinger. Let's not land her with that. Let's not land either of them with that. Both, in fact, I would say, consistently displayed a commendable get-up-and-go.

But, to the event. We return here to 'the master of the art'. It was known that — among his accomplishments — he could transform himself at the click — or without the click — of a finger, turn himself into anything he pleased. Bee, salmon, bat, stallion, yellow-hammer, flamingo. Gazelle. But she'd never seen him perform the miracle. Naturally she was curious, hungry even.

—You've never done it for me.
—That's true.
—Well, will you?
—No.
—Why not?
—I told you. If I do it — and anything goes wrong — then

that's it. *Kaput.*
　—How could anything go wrong?
　—Because we live in the world.
　—Need it be *our* world?
　—Listen to me, will you —
　—I'm listening.
　—You're talking dangerous energies here, you're talking a fierce *charge* — things can very easily go wrong. Understand?
　She nodded but she didn't understand, not one bit, why should she? Would you? Over quite a period, accordingly, she kept up the pressure. She wanted him, quite simply, to do it for *her.*
　—I want you to do it for *me*, that's all.
　—You've told me.
　—I'm not sure I made it clear to you though —
　—Make it clear to me then.
　—Sometimes I think I don't know you at all.
　—Yes?
　—Sometimes I think that I'll never know you — but that's all right — it's something else that matters —
　—What?
　—I want to *understand* you — that's a different matter — I just want to *understand* you . . .
　In the end, he relented.
　—All right, I'll do it — but on conditions.
　—Conditions?
　—Yes — I can't do it except on conditions.
　—What are the conditions?
　—Conditions are that you submit yourself to three tests of your nerve.
　—Ah . . .
　—What do you mean 'Ah . . . '?
　—I'm not to be trusted — apparently.
　—Of course I trust you — but that's not the point.
　—What is the point?
　—The point is — as I've told you a thousand times — that in a matter as dicey as this every precaution must be taken.
　—Should I insure you?
　—It's not a joking matter, you know.
　—Don't fret, I treat it as seriously as you.
　—So you agree to the conditions?

—Of course, I agree.
—Fine —
—And good-luck.
—To us both.

They were in the livingroom, a fine summer evening, window open, clear sound of the river — the Dodder, as a matter of fact — which flowed just about right by the house. He clicked a finger.

Nothing happened. He smiled. She smiled. They were both — already — enjoying the keenest sense of a dance — a duel — going on. He clicked a finger again — but this time he was merely pretending the click. They both laughed out loud. And the laughter made lucidly audible a wonderful sizzle of tension in the room.

Now: he clicked a finger — for real. Water poured in the window — the river, in short, obediently raised itself, and commenced to flood the room. Flooded the room. The furniture, once afloat — delighted with this novel element — began to spin about anarchically. Chairs, lamps, tv dinner-tables, tv, all delivered themselves to the caper like kids at the shallow end of the pool. The much-loved maidenhair fern took off with a triple bow. Ashtrays coasted the waters in the guise of exhausted ballroom dancers.

—What's sometimes referred to as an *inundation*, she offered.

They looked at each other. The water was at her décolletage, and rising. Now at her throat. Now tipping her chin. Approaching her lips. 'It loves your red lips,' an imp in him urged the comment — but he held back, watched her unwaveringly. She remained quite extraordinarily calm, casual even. He clicked a finger. The waters receded.

—One down, he allowed himself.

—Two to go, she grinned — game for anything, really.

As happens in such cases, the room — on the spot — was dry as snuff. The contestants — likewise. The furniture exactly back in position, and going on about its stabilising duties, asserting propriety in that decently inaudible murmur which is the inheritance of furniture wherever it may be. Everything was fine. Until the next hullabaloo — which, naturally, was imminent.

Again he clicked a finger. It was six o'clock on a summer evening, that sepia-tinted eternal summer evening, and in through the same window-opening — the angelus tolling stolidly, piquant counterpoint that drew from her a half-smile — in through the window comes a serpent.

A curiosity of serpents: they always seem to have come up out of the ground. Or the lake. So with this specimen. She registered that — effect — at once. Beyond that, you'd say, neither ghastly nor mundane. Just — a serpent. Ten metres of it. Wait. Fifteen. Foot thick. They both watched.

The serpent, eyes lidless *à la mode*, colour a potent mix of *lie-de-vin* and terra cotta, settled in felicitous coils by the window. But not for long. Towards her in a choreographed lurch — the sense of contained force a shock to her circulation — and, same impetus, starts winding about her, ankles, knees, groin, at an easy impudent pace.

He was standing about four metres away, watching her, watching the action. She kept her eyes directly on him, the viewer, but that didn't prevent her from assimilating the action. The serpent's head was already lolling against her breasts. She could feel a cold hum from within the beast. And the whiff of *terra incognita*. Suction, better.

Stasis. She had the sense of the serpent — now motionless — listening to her. Gathering all her secrets. From his vantage point by the sideboard, the perpetrator of all this — but she'd asked for it, fair enough, insisted — he, master of the art, held her eyes. Cold non-aroma of the serpent. A cloak about her. A wall. She drove back a rictus of panic, tilted her defiant brow.

—You're a credit.

—Me — or the beast?

He clicked a finger. The serpent left, same route, flowed out of the room like the perfectly-trained servant in one of those Wilde plays. She listened for a plop in the river. None came.

—How're you doing?

—How do you think I'm doing?

He clicked a finger again. The door opened and a woman entered. The cousin from the West. Dead ten years. Close friends, he, she, this visitor from — somewhere else. The visitor walked right up to her in the middle of the room, looked into her. Into her face. Her eyes. Into her. A lost confident look, it seemed to the recipient. Inimitable. Not of the earth.

—How are you, Helen? she asked the visitor.

No answer. Same steady look.

—Speak to me, Helen.

No answer.

He clicked a finger. The visitor left the room, same route, same soundless path. Gone. He looked at her. Smiling. Ready. Not eager. But ready.

—Good, he said, want a rest or —

—Do I look as if I want a rest?

Perhaps it was he who needed the rest. He strolled to the piano, stood leaning against it for a full two minutes, studying a sheepskin rug by his feet. Next thing he was gone, and there was a blackbird flying proprietorially about the room. A couple of feet from the ceiling. Repeated circling, using the maximum diameter available. Warm sheen of the plumage, pristine yellow of the bill. Eyes alert, knowing, tender. The bird was recognisable — and unrecognisable.

She watched — swivelling — the blackbird in flight. In her watching discern the light of a woman in love. Watching her, not watching, the bird continued flying in the same resiliently controlled pattern. Blackbird in love? Why not? The room was brimming love. Sound of the river. Primrose haze now to the evening. She laughed to herself. To the bird. She wanted to sing.

Now a fresh rhythm. The bird was narrowing the diameter of the circle, decisively, coming closer to her, at the same time descending in measured curves. Now the bird was directly above her, hovering. She could hear — filmy — the wing-beat. Then, the lightest touch, she felt the bird land on her left shoulder.

At that moment she was facing the window above the river and she didn't turn her head. She kept her eyes on the bay-laurel which graced the garden but to the bird her body gave welcome. And registered a response she could never describe, then or later. A reciprocal — something. Tickle.

Beat. Three beats. And the bird began to sing. Song flowed from the pulsing throat of the bird and into the room, the characteristic bountiful song of the blackbird, the notes full, unstinting. The song filled the room, and then — natural progression — filled her, invaded her, swept along her veins, alarmed flesh and bone with a touch now pussy-willow, now purling silk, took her away, and asked for nothing in return — bar the listening.

The pure song of the blackbird, she told herself — and others — afterwards, but there was more to it than that, it was that plus a melodic sub-song, thread that kept transforming the silver of the notes to gold. And the gold was love. And the price you pay. And untrammeled deference to that buoyant equation.

No telling how long it lasted. Eyes vaguely on the garden foliage, she saw the cat — pampered calico stranger — slope through the window to sit primly by the piano. Had she imagined that 'primly'? The bird-song owned her. Recklessly it poured. The cat sprang. Her arms shot up to protect the bird. And she fainted.

When she came to what struck her at once was the silence. There was no sign of the bird. No sign of the cat. On the sheepskin rug a single wing-feather.

The feather was given a place of honour in the room. Set on a white saucer, a glass bowl covering the saucer. The feather was cherished, watched, that is, as it crinkled, shrivelled piecemeal, and, in the ripeness of time, became a strand of dust.

One day the saucer is empty. Perhaps there's a smudge.

The saucer resumes its place with the rest of the delph. It's workaday again. Anonymous under your cup of tea. Sugar? Milk? Summer evening. What tree is that, would you say? Bird-song. Cool stir of the river.

The Word for Yes

I was spending a little time in hospital. Not unexpectedly, he arrived. There's something of the born visitor to him.

Lip hanging like a side of bacon, he chose a cool distance. I thought it useful to fire first.

—You're pure nineteenth-century melodrama.

He offered a distempered grin, spoke in his ambiguous bear's paw of a voice.

—Baa-baa, black sheep, have you any wool?

I rose like barm.

—Yes, Sir, yes, Sir, *three* bags full. *One* for the master, *one* for the Maid, and *one* for the Little Boy who lives down the lane.

He left. I lay back, jubilant. This once, at any rate, I'd gone through him for a short cut.

We didn't meet for a long time. Who was avoiding whom? No idea. Take that back. We were avoiding each other. Qualify that. I was avoiding him, can't speak for the related proposition.

Why avoiding him? For the same reason that you, friend, on sound general principles avoid certain pushy specimens among your intimates.

We met again in Leningrad — made sense to me. On February 14th — that too made sense. Associations? St Valentine's Day massacre, Al Capone, wasn't it? Plus a much deeper association touching a woman who eluded me. Of which more later. Maybe.

(She was a high-flier, that much I'll vouchsafe. And she had company up there, the entire Fleet Air-Arm, if truth be told.)

Anyway. Leningrad. Valentine's Day. Early hours of Valentine's Day. Often called the *small* hours, a misnomer, surely. Aren't they, as a rule, spacey, sprawling, leached of the finite?

We're in a large ballroom, the pair of us. We have it to ourselves, own it. The floor is marble, lozenged black-and-white. That design belatedly intrigues me — but let it pass.

We're waltzing, to no music but our own, as the poets say. Waltzing, however, on the horizontal. Sliding, better perhaps. Sliding/whizzing about the highly polished marble floor in a close horizontal embrace.

Like two perilously sober drunks.

The embrace is sufficiently close, controlled, to prevent me ever seeing his face. That's an urge, by the way. Not a necessity. I can smell who it is.

We spin about the floor. He — I concede now, conceded then — is the one in charge.

We could be there yet but, no doubt, he had other things to be doing. The whirl came to a stop, my head in close proximity to his loins. And I'm looking at his bared privates, scrotum tight, cock erect.

Some weeks later we met in Moscow. Arbat Street. No, I'm making that up. Wish it had been — Arbat so textured — but no. Some street or other, centre of the city, dusk.

The circumstances were, as often (it will be apparent) in our meetings, *louche*.

Dusk, as I say. Heavy traffic. And I'm strolling along naked. The evening is unseasonably mild. I don't say that in self-justification but it was. Nobody in the least bothered (*pro tem*) by my naked state. Except me. I admit to unease. Edginess.

So what was the rationale? There was none. All I can say — I'm being quite open — is that I so behave at irregular intervals. Undress. Go for a walk. A run.

Arbat Street then — or whatever street it was. I'm becoming antsy about my exposed pelt. This fret has congealed to a burden when a passing motorist, male, nondescript — your average guy trying to turn a rouble, *à la mode* among the Muscovites — pulls over, waves me in.

I get into the back. No words exchanged — there is the language problem. I find a pullover on the seat, and make free to requisition it. Solace of the gansy. In far foreign fields.

The car proceeds.

While you'd wink, checkpoint up ahead. At speed, it's our turn. I glimpse the face of the one — *the* one of the pair — manning the barrier. Oh, yes. The driver lets down the window.

A head-and-shoulders fills it. And a coiled arm. There's no hesitation, plainly I'm expected. The coiled arm uncoils, extends itself with supple authority. The hand collects mine, pulls it forward, crisply checks it against the driver's.

He's not slow, say that for him.

I found myself liking him more. Warming, cagily, to his sense of humour. Incipient, at least. But meanwhile we remained strangers. And at odds.

The question, as always, who'd now make the move?

Recently I was compelled to change house. I found an apartment overlooking a park. I'd scarcely moved in when, glancing out the window one evening, I see him directly opposite, among the trees, looking right up at me, my abode.

The alacrity shocked me.

The audacity.

And brought us, once more that little bit closer. His demeanour among the trees? Watchful, yes. But what else? Bit lost. Standing there under the trees.

More precisely, I had the sense he was showing me his face. Offering it, could be.

It will be evident we're moving towards a rendezvous.

Sabbath rendezvous, I've felt for some days. Something to do with Sunday quiet. Something to do with us, the pair of us. Merely a hunch.

But on Sundays expect to find in me a special state of waiting.

I amble to the window to check the park. Sunlit. Deserted. Too early in the day for much activity. Nip in the air.

I focus on a particular tree, tall healthy fir. And, as if in abeyance for my eye, action.

Among the topmost branches, a horse and rider appear. Next, horse and rider float fluidly down through the branches — causing hardly a stir, land below, and set off across the park in a confident canter. And quickly out of my vision.

Held by the window, I'm aware there's someone beside me.

Second spectator. I know it's he.
 I turn to him. His drawn eyes. Still on the park.
 —Who was that? I ask.
 —The bridegroom.
 —And the bride?
 He doesn't reply.
 —I want to know you.
 —I know.
 He looks directly at me.
 Your breath is stained, I think. Mine too. I catch the noise of some woeful episode in deeps of the forest.
 —All right?
 —Right.
 We strip for the encounter.
 No handshake.
 It begins.

Rise Up Lovely Sweeney

What do I want? I want to know. I want to know what ish my nation? What ish my nation? Too much to ask. My nation is Appalachia, Appalachia, worn trail of eye for hand, tooth for claw, scalp for cup and saucer, busted telly in the bog-hole, washing-machine sneezing rust on the uninsurable bargain-line, *Listen*, listen for the wind through the nuts and bolts, listen — Excuse me! Excuse-a me! May I answer my questions? I hear no talk of Baby — she is not mentioned. We keep Baby in the fridge, cool clear sound when she jingles, her eyes, believe it, a snow sky, not a hyacinth, not a tint, tall blue of the garlic never-no-more, and in the towns — rattle the banger and give her stick — in the dead-march towns I see marooned mom-to-be lamenting last year's laughter, look at her, belle of the local, perched before the one-arm sweepstake, cloud of peanuts her only prayer — while the arcades spit and stutter like the Sea of Tranquillity under a poxy equinoctial moon and the crouched young put their heads away with galactic zippity-dooh-dah . . . Do you mind? Bush in the gap, please. Were you born in a field? It's too long a war, she grows old, grey the gills, creaky windpipe, dew the tattered smig — who will cry sweetness, cancel black confetti, come home by night, kiss the Wet Gate, lavabo there and laugh till morning? All right. All right. *All right*. Wash me in the water where you wash your dirty daughter — could I speak more plainly? — that, repeat, is this merchant's pulse of yearning, bathe me in the water where you wash your dirty daughter — but you won't, you won't, *you will not do it*. What? *What?* Clearly, please — the static's user-friendly if you soothe it, play it, ride it, inside of the knees. Yes? The heart's needle? We have met, no daw she, and therefore let her flow, glow, succinctly glide, she knows where benison resides, let her flow, abide instruction, take sweet Baby from the fridge, air the house, fumigate the floors, *Hold your hammer tongues will you?* Where was I? Cue . . . Cue, please . . . Cue . . . House, thank-you . . . House, floors, correct, fumigate, and meet the question: why have they hidden trust? And where may I find it? White of an egg? The shoe-box smell? Under the ashtray? You tell me, cable collect, round the globe or across the ice, 'phone me, fax me, lick me, brave me on the slope of scalp for scalp, cup for saucer, broken road of we leaf-people — how much do you weigh? State your weight. You? You? You? Are you refusing witness — leaf-people numberless as autumn or the whine oh that whine in the chair when night comes . . . *Entendu* . . . You do not perhaps credit the hurt mind? I remember one morning a disc in the sky. That sun or moon? Speak, someone . . . I can't tell sun from moon, can't tell sun from moon . . . .

—We'll find you, Sweeney — because you want to be found. That's your stick, friend. You want to be found. If we didn't exist you'd have to compose us, you really would. You wouldn't know what to do with your resonating spoor, friend, and a man must know what to do with his resonating spoor, right?

The Interrogator and he were nothing if not mutually conversable, they loved that joust — among other jousts, 'phone the preferred mode, both gave 'good 'phone' — perversely spiced, as will be apparent.

—Yes?
—How are we today, Sweeney?
—Never better.
—Sweeney?
—Yes . . .
—Care to help the friends of the enemy?
—And they so in need.
—Sweeney?
—Yes . . .
—You scratch my back I'll scratch yours.
—Can't wait.
—Other ways we can help.
—Like ould times.
—No one to know.

—Naturally.
—Except you.
—To be sure.
—And us.
—Toes to the fire.
—Think about it, Sweeney.
—It will be given —
—All due —
—Con-sider-ay-shun.
—Sweeney?
—Yes. . .
—I'm talking seriously. You need something. We need something. You scratch my back. I scratch yours. All quietly. Other ways we can help. No one to know. Except you. And us. Think about it.

What is it about institutional noises, so insidiously porous, and carrying — by decree, it would appear — that neural whiff of formaldehyde, ether, stewed tea, and spurned vegetable soup? Immemorial whirrings from the walls, crisp steps on tile or parquet, in every alcove a sculpted Cerberus wheezing final orders, and, dominating for the moment, inter-com crackle and message — *Calling Doctor Shevlin . . . Emergency . . . Calling Doctor Shevlin . . . Will Doctor Shevlin please come at once to Recreation . . . Will Doctor Shevlin please come at once to Recreation . . . Thank-you . . .* Clang prolonged of a bell, lift noises, trolley noises, song of the cistern, the inter-com again, attend — *Will patients please note, Television Room open three pm to midnight or possibly longer every day this week . . .* Roger, no, charged pause, you can smell it, Parthian coda, thar she blows — *Pending notice to the contrary . . .*
Sweeney took it all in one ear, demeanour of the half-reared rabbit but in heaps of the deeps undismayed as, once again oh ye nettles and thistles of the downy sward, he stabbed his calculator, watched the digits flow.
—Ounce of blood . . . Ounce of blood before the churn of buttermilk . . . Blood all over . . . What do I want? I want your blue eye . . . Your fair right hand? Of course. Thank you very much, that's very thoughtful of you indeed . . . .
He laughed to himself, harrow in there somewhere, keep well

clear or, at any rate, ponder discretion.

—An island — consider carefully — an island, after all, is a barometer *par excellence* — *BUT* — I hear no talk of the heart's needle. Not a single solitary word. That needle floats. She's mobile. *Mo-bile*. Don't forget either the bad day. We have graves that eat flowers like pigs at the trough. *I want to be the man with no skin.*

About him gabble and din of his companions, he tuned in at intervals, reminded him of — he foraged — Monteverdi, no earlier than that, choristers of the gargoyle, mayhap, the mélange often tilting, as now, to a litany of sorts, repetition — here above all — *pia mater studiorum* but never sufficient, naturally.

—Calm yourself Paddy, you're a bundle of nerves.

—Mungavin was here but he's now back in prison thank God.

—You'll never milk a cow again bhoy.

—What ish my nayshun? My nayshun is the howl but not the black howl... Some say the whinge, I say the howl — but not the black howl.

—Ah Jaysus don't shoot me don't shoot me the Mammy'll kill me.

Sweeney threw in his tuppence-worth, his best *missa cantata* counter-tenor rattling the large (mercifully reeded) panes.

—Jesus stabs Ireland in the north, south, and south south-east by south.

Stutter of applause — or was it for the Matron? — just arrived in Recreation. Collar and cuffs shone, rebarbative. Large salient eyes swept the throng.

—Not a smile. Not one smile. And this in an era when it's scientifically accepted that people who go around smiling all the time feel happier because the smiles are triggering happy brain chemicals. And we all know — oh too well we know — the sourpusses who not only frown all the time but are bad company besides. They make themselves dreary by looking dreary, isn't that right, Sweeney?

—Madame?

—Answer my question.

—Madame?

—*Sweeney* —

—All I ever wanted was to walk across a field.

—And pluck watercress from the stream — the familiar plaint.

—Madame, do not mock that greeny hansel.
—Do I mock, Sweeney?
And rippled her haunches. Sweeney stood the ground.
—I know the why of the watercress. I know the reason. The cause of the reason.
—*Up any down whatever!*
An intruder, centre-left, *con brio*. Mayhem the aspiration, mayhem granted. Short-lived. The concert must go on. And Matron confiding in her walkie-talkie. With intent. Hands shot up here and there, a pattern. The apple-polishers.
—Patient O'Brien, you'd your hand up first, I believe.
O'Brien rose, ingratiating as a cow on a cock of hay.
—Matron, I read in a book — and do believe — that the chronically low-spirited may be made to feel more cheerful if given the right facial exercises — such as being forced to smile frequently. This theory — if valid — as I believe it to be — could benefit huge numbers, including manic depressives, social misfits, unsuccessful sales-persons, and jilted lovers, to name but a few.
—You can't tell the measure till you pour, can you?
Sweeney. Who else?
—*Can you?*
Taking Sweeney in and keeping him out, Matron addressed herself to little Nurse Kangley, not the worst, a yard to her right.
—Nurse?
—Matron?
—Appetite?
—He'd ate the head of a horse, Matron.
—Pulse?
—Ate a farmer's arse to a bush, Matron.
—*Pulse?*
Oh — hoppin' up and down like an egg in a ponger, Matron.
—Stool?
—Not a gig, Matron.
—Sleep?
—Like a corpse, Matron.
—Thank-*you.*
Sweeney lifted, clamorous.
—*I want to be the man with no skin.*
Matron was wearing her white tolerances that morning and a good job too. When she spoke her voice undulated the equilib-

rium of the true professional.

—Your home is in the east, Sweeney, not the west, you know that perfectly well.

Little Nurse Kangley had started to sing, trick she had, light into it anywhere, in the family, some asserted, distaff side. Anyway, country-and-western —

—*Eatin' another man's bread / Climbin' another man's stair...*

Positively Dantean, Sweeney ticked, on the banks of the Ar-ni-o...

Matron hummed to her own clock.

—It's a good, Sweeney, to distinguish the cardinal points. We have innumerable books here on the subject.

And still the maiden sang...

—*And askin' the stars of the night / If they know the words of a prayer...*

—I remember, Sweeney, *nel mezzo*, goaded Her Ladyship, I remember one morning walking across fields.

She rose to it.

—We're back to his watercress — Jeeez-*us*.

And out the door in flitters, little Kangley thread in the slipstream.

Sweeney gladly turned to his neighbour and next-of-kin — a problematic figure whom Sweeney, for that reason, called *Die Brocken*. Or on his garrulous days, *Brocken, I hardly knew ye*.

Spoke to this — creation, handling answer as well as question with filleted aplomb.

—Ever feel like a fist? Yes, indeed... A fist around smoke? Ah ... catch question ... State your position. The black lake has disturbed you? Well, why not say so to commence?

The house looked like a place that had once been home. Sweeney spat into the decorum of the lupins, clear the gullet of nostalgia before it could curdle his spit. He felt fine but knew the law: never feel all right when you feel all right. Rang the bell. Chimes — marzipan frangipane, and then some. Rang again. Light in the hall. Her steps. *Ecce mulier*.

—Jesus Christ...

—Or his first cousin once removed.

—Where'd you come from?

—Am I asked in, dear wife?

—Dyin' to be turned away?

He entered, closed the door on a snarl of wind, scud of rain. Followed her along the hall to the kitchen. Her shoulders *en garde*, the liver of her courage and the kidneys of her valour. Had its attractions. The kitchen.

—Take the weight off your bones.

—Had to come by.

Healthy odour of cooking, rice dominant. Sweet-and-sour sauce there somewhere. He took his old chair, Captain's Chair, knew at once he'd lost the fit of it.

—Get you something?

Her *politesse* moue.

—Had to come by.

—Whispered you were on your travels.

He enjoyed teasing her the bit.

—To look, to see, to know.

—We're watched.

—We're all watched — from the first slither. All's watched.

—Cup of something?

—Half a mouthful in the hand.

She prepared coffee, relaxing minutely. Rain swept the window. The fridge grumbled. He rose, stuffed a wad of newspaper into its rere innards. She watched, not watching. The fridge quieted. He sat again, bent himself to the sociable.

—Just parted from Mungavin.

—How's he?

—The philosopher of the outfit. He'd remind you of a clock with the mange. Bits he gets right. That chin on him like the heel of a gate.

—Try that.

—And the lip hanging like a side of bacon. Thanks.

He took the coffee. Knew the mug. Didn't recognise the coffee. The 'phone rang in the hall. She left, answered it. Female friend, his antennae pronounced, from the colour of scraps drifting. Mungavin came back to him, connoisseur of the woeful the same Mungavin, morose statistician of ways and means, across millennia.

—You're right, Mungavin. We could never kill with their finesse. They work like surgeons, we like butchers. Same with torture. They operate, we hack and tear. Poison likewise. With us

strychnine, arsenic, weedkiller. Nod with them, wink, tip your shoe. Their deed never is, our every move a blossoming stain.
  —Talking to yourself?
He shook off Mungavin.
  —Terrible coffee. Tastes of me Ould Skilara Hat.
  —Sup of whiskey?
  —Be a help.
She produced the Black Bush, poured him a belt, helped herself. They sipped, no toast, that season by.
  —Something to sing to you.
  —Go ahead, Luciano.
Weather at the window, pulse of the wedding-present clock — punitive sentry from the word *Go*, and — only now he noticed — thin purr of radiomuzak from under the newspaper on the chair to his left.
  —*Tying your hair behind / Or hovering to kiss / Or caught in the window / Fringe hiding your eyes / You're the dancer, aren't you? . . . Sway like the one / Tip-top of the tree / And kissed by the sun . . . I remember that kiss / Light wand of your lips . . .*
She studied the cooker. Fraught.
  —Light wand of your lips . . .
And Sweeney — resolution up the chimney — could not resist the dander down *La Rue Passéiste*.
  —You remember?
  —Yes, I remember.
Two to fandango, knew he could rely on her.
  —You do?
  —Course I remember.
  —What?
  —Your hands . . . Smell . . . Laughing in your sleep . . . What you said the day I asked, How's it you always look so naked?
  —What'd I say?
  —'An illusion . . . Just an illusion . . . '
Pause. He was nearing the garden where the praties grow. And in bad times fester.
  —And him?
  —What about him?
  —A fast mover.
  —They're thick on the ground.
  —One of your busy bees.

—'Busy'?
—All the juice he can suck.
—We talk mostly of you.
—Thanks.
—You I want.
—We two on the run?
—I want you.
—Nest in the ditch?
—You're famished . . .
—The road for a grave.
—Stay here tonight.
—You don't suss it, he viewed her through the *dubia* of his flighty aspirations, I'm for the wood. There's a tree in there that's cradle and coffin and all between.

Sough in the rafters, one he remembered. And sough again. Thank-you, prodigious nature. In the hammock of sough-on-sough, they took their ease, unease, together, not touching.

—You've gone by me, Sweeney.

She looking into him, cross-hatching his *Requiescat*. He bore no grudge. He'd need favouring winds, all the prayers. He perked.

—Sweeney's Hallowed First Law? The more you free yourself from projections the more others project on to you. Sweeney's Crooked Second? The more you free yourself from projections the more others project on to you the more you project on to others . . . .

—Sweeney's Wise Third?

—Not yet formulated. No, wait — just now formulated. Sweeney's Wise Third: you see more with the glimpse.

—Are you all right?

She looked frightened.

—Never was. Didn't you map it in my eyes? Footin' it in hailstones, mind always on early departure.

He rose, kissed her lightly.

—Ciao, bella.

She followed him down the hall as he melted through the door and into the night. The rough night to be. Shadow on the footpath. Gone.

—You're cracked, Sweeney, she gripped the door, y'know that, pure cracked.

With Matling there was no danger of transference. That was plus one. And the game — by definition — was on Sweeney's turf. Plus two. And Matling belonged, seed and breed, to the other crowd, Queen's English his cradle lisp and adult ticket-of-leave. But no match for Sweeney there, Sweeney would always be ahead in that contest.

—Do you have a sense, Matling pushed off, sometimes I feel this is what you're saying — do you have a sense of — almost deliberately — leaving tracks — to help him in the pursuit?

—Sometimes.

—Sometimes?

The squaring-up had commenced. *Très aimable*, Sweeney feinted with the left.

—Look, don't we all leave tracks — willy-nilly? Come to that, don't we all *want* to leave tracks?

—Especially if we know the pursuer...

—Especially if the pursuer's an intimate.

—'Intimate'?

The questioner, leisurely, note on his scratch-pad.

—Symbiotic, isn't it?

—Rapidly that?

—With such as him — and such as me — yes.

—Do you like him?

—I don't have likes — or dislikes.

Matling, without looking up, bowed, salute (presumably) towards Sweeney's iridescent halo. The boat rocked gently. Sweeney saw a pike, jack-pike in trim, flow past, intent. Another tack.

—Describe being on the run?

—Lord Clarendon — sometime in the eighteenth century — got it half-right, Sweeney blossomed, inflexions orotund, Horatian the tilt of his eye, 'There's a narrow pass in East Cavan where, upon enquiry, every man becomes a bush, and every bush a Tory'.

—'Tory'?

—Outlaw. Dispossessed.

The scratch-pad again. Under 'curious usages of the natives', safely assume. Sweeney delayed in the eighteenth century. The speck of island they were approaching — the boat allowed to drift — had been fashioned by Swift, no less. As a practical joke.

Probably meant to disappear. Was disappearing. *Ave*, Jonathan, *moriturus te salutat*.

—Sometimes the English use English wonderfully well, don't you think? Such clarity . . . We use language for . . .

—Camouflage?

Very good, Matling.

—What else?

A silence then, the boat going down the lake with the breeze, sou'-west, to lodge comfortably in the reeds which bordered the bog. A heron lifted, exuding affront, and vanished beyond trees. They came to the main business, appetites up, the day that was in it, heft of the theme, and sweeter the meat nearer the bone.

—Were you surprised when you found him sleeping in that room?

—Not at all.

—Why not?

—Because a side of me, Sweeney fondled a rowlock to his right, always expected to be taken while sleeping. So why shouldn't that happenstance — probability — law — or whatever it is — why shouldn't it also apply to him? Why shouldn't *he* be taken sleeping in the place — on the couch — where I slept yesterday? If he's *that* much on your trail he's bound sometime or other to fall into your bed . . . Maybe he knows his *posture* — that intimate venue — somehow guarantees preservation — maybe he knows that?

Reflective doodling. Terse.

—In the event it did?

—I looked down at him, Sweeney nodded, and my first thought was, Christ, does he have to snore like that? That meant he was safe.

—Because?

—I was seeing him as human. Next thing — naturally — I wanted to blow his head off. That passed. Then I was moved to address him. Not moved — compelled — I'd no choice.

—You spoke to him?

Matling's wondering smile, his best poem.

—I whispered, 'The soil exceptionally sticky, water has difficulty finding a way out'. Description of the hills, drumlin country, we're both from. It's a running gag we share.

—Then he woke up?

—His eyes opened.

—Your eyes met?
—The peepers met.
—An exchange?
—I believe he was still asleep . . . Yes, one of our great exchanges. Only about ten seconds — then his eyes closed again, easy as a child's. And, like that, he's snoring fit to scutch flax. It came to me, we're playing tig the pair of us but the bullets are for real. Then I left. The snores followed me down the path.

The breeze had nudged the boat so that they were enveloped by the reeds, reredos of wan ochre hugging them, and susurrus of insect life. A heron next time round, Sweeney thought. Comical bird. Stare at his reflection, the moon high.

—That was it? Matling resumed.
—Almost. Suddenly I was furious I hadn't left a token — some sign — I have this streak of the act*or* in me. A moment. I realised no sign could match the meeting. Our spoors had blended. No call to ham.
—And that was it?
—Almost.

The antiphonal eddy tickled both.

—I bumped into Mungavin. Told him the whole story. We turned and went back to that house — with a certain caution — and itchy fingers. I'm susceptible, open to every wind that blows. Of course he was gone.

Reflect. That ye may be made whole. Relish the silence, the spaces it possesseth. And they did, there in their veil of ochre. And, if not made whole, were not made bits of. That would come. Let it.

—What was that quotation again?
Quilca, from *cuilceach*, 'abounding in reeds' . . .
—Your Lord Clarendon quote?
—*There's a narrow pass*, Sweeney *ore rotundo*, head lolling on oak of the bow, *There's a narrow pass in East Cavan where upon enquiry —*
—*Every man becomes a bush —*
—*And every bush a Tory.*
They could be there yet.

Odours of the wood, and sounds of the wood — approved, quotidian, with, close-up, the sounds of Sweeney's withershins advance, ragged steps, chesty crepitations, slivers of invective . . . He was enjoying himself, with the usual reservations. Substantial solace to him the sound of the bittern — officially banished from these parts but *boom-boom* far from, far from *boom-boom*, and, hard by that, belling of the stags, glaze in the eye and sweat on those loins.

—Antlers under the moon, he paused in the silky purlieus of a white alder, there's a sign, you that's one for signs.

Onward. Focus on the triple-phase of breathing. Lower abdomen. Solar plexus. Thorax. The oxygen of — self-habitation. And a name. Explore.

—Who knows the know? There's one for you. Who knows the know? Why, the Man with No Skin, me ould segotia, he knows the know. Yes — *but* — 'But me no buts' — has he anything to say? Oh yes, certainly, no mute he. So what does he say? He says as follows, and, really, it's enough to bleed hairpins, he says, says he, *Know the answer, still say nothing, your head'll explode*. Shall I repeat? Please . . . Says the Man with No Skin, our lost next of kin, *Know the answer, still say nothing, your head'll explode*.

A hen-pheasant, *embonpoint*, took off from long grass to his left, and a man stepped from behind a fir adjacent.

—Who're you, mate?

—A madman.

Sweeney took a long drag of him. Salt-smell from the sweat of canter. Body sound as a pebble. Face the leavings of synthetic cubism.

—Shake.

—All the time.

They both laughed, fret in the selvage.

—Where you coming from?

—Where I left.

—Where you bound for?

—Where I'm going.

Snookered, Sweeney grinned. *Boom-boom* of the bittern. The madman alerted, vouchsafed.

—There's one of the rare ould stock.

—The lad with the trumpet.

—What's he sounding now?

—Looking for his oats.

This risqué grace-note set the madman warbling *entre guillemets*.

—Is it the call I'm seeking?

The clear sound of a rifle-shot nipped the pair. Sweeney stirred his shadow, enquired.

—Long to go?

—Be dead in a month.

—You've had the word?

—Saw my face in a waterfall.

—The worst sign.

—How'll you go?

—Bullet through the left nipple. A quiet morning. Soon.

Impudent seductive woodwind and brass of the bittern again. And the madman's fluent face agreeing (*pro tem*) with Pablo: *You can't be a witch-doctor twenty-four hours a day.* Sweeney liked this vagrant.

—What drove you mad?

—Forgotten. A woman. A man. Forgotten.

—'A man, a woman. A woman, a man. Forgotten,' acquisitive Sweeney edited, put a shine on, knife that on the stone.

And the madman was gone.

Thereafter water, Calvary, and listening to the timber. As the madman evaporated, the stream-sound impinged, the clatter of 'copters fought it, the whole fleet, they moved on, the stream again. He could sniff an ally, a comforter, a stay.

—The greeny hansel.

He was by the stream, he was on his knees, reaching, plucking the cress.

—*Un morceau, s'il vous plait* . . . Pure protein . . .

He guzzled, green about the mouth, taste-buds opening to a strop in the juice. It was like eating colour, the colour of now.

—What'd you be doing at your long table with your curly cabbage and your hairy bacon?

The mother had always called it 'water-grass', her voice an endearment above it. He was aware that Pliny gave *Nasturtium Officinale* — 'nose-twister' — but he begged leave, even as he chewed, to advance 'that which longs for wet soil'. From the Greek. Whether or which — he rose, wiping the gob with the back of his hand — no plant richer on the brown mountains of the world.

The Calvary cameo was — as ever — unexpected, and ineluctable. His diary entry — he'd often thought of keeping one but just as often settled, the convenience of it, for the palimpsest of memory, those seething ambages — but had there been a diary entry, thus the copperplate, raindrops on the page, the muddy thumb-mark, field-report unassailable —

> The top of a tall ivied hawthorn. Every twist a dose of the nine-tails. Roost elsewhere, fair traveller. In sight under the old moon thicket of briars swollen with waiting, single blackthorn in the middle rising clear and clarion. To the tip of the blackthorn. The blackthorn holds, sways, holds. The blackthorn gives. All thorns needle and tear. Floor of the thicket. Skin pumping. Warm ooze of the blood.

Not exactly a bath of milk, courtesy of the Exuberant One. However, towards the diminution of the dove-grey hours, the bird on the shoulder unforecastably sang.

—Oak? Two acorns floating, stirred by the wind . . . Elder? Necklace of nine berries a cure . . . Pine? Crane roosting within . . . Beech? Thin boards for the secret song . . . Aspen? Why should we tremble? Ash, elm, sycamore, birch, hazel, blackthorn, yewy yew . . . Fir? Eat before dawn the seeds of that cone . . . .

Sweeney listened, scholar Sweeney or, better, at last out and about, meeting the scholars and them coming home, Sweeney listened, prayed, listened, listened, prayed he might be granted the know of the trees.

—Inspector, Inspector — I'll sing the Song of Songs for twenty cigarettes. Entire New Testament for a bottle of Bush — I mean it, Inspector. I kid you not, kiddo . . . .

The Inspector, smiling acknowledgement, did not break stride. Taking modest satisfaction in the modest authority of his steps descending the stone stairway, he looked forward with modest anticipation to this evening's foursome. Meanwhile, he was awaited. A friend was waiting.

Doors innumerable purred, video-eyes gleamed recognition, and he had arrived at the Maximum Security Section. A silent lively place. From *Cell 40* — busy venue over the past few days — the up-an'-at-'em of an Irish jig, *The Cow that Ate the Piper*, whipcrack across it at regular intervals, and the wallop of lunatic step-dancing, one performer, the renowned Kelly, Detective Inspector Orr conducting, the father an organist, taught music at Methody.

Cell 55. One button for the electronic control. And there was Sweeney. The Inspector shut the door quietly.

—Sit down, Prisoner Sweeney.

Standing by the bed, paperback in hand, Sweeney made no move to comply.

—I'm bigger stannin' like a dog sittin'.

The Inspector slapped him across the lug. Sweeney sat.

The Inspector strolled the cell, a cool warm-up exercise, for, say, two minutes. The Inspector halted. Looked at Sweeney, durable on the bed. The Inspector fired.

—Ever wash, Sweeney? Scrub? Loose the loofah? Deodorize? Spell soap? Can you add, Sweeney? Use a calculator? What's a square? A T-square? A parallel line? Ever work, Sweeney? Walk straight? Use a condom? Look someone in the eye? Buy your own round? Hit the sack sober? Shave without a shake?

The Inspector's colleagues arrived in twos and threes. Five minutes later there was a choir of ten active, hurling the questions — the same set of questions — from shifting angles, at shifting speeds, in shifting registers, tempestuous chorale.

—*Durate e servate rebus secundis*, Sweeney invoked, mute the while.

The only bit of Virgil he knew, it had often given support.

After fifteen minutes — this was a guess, Sweeney was without a watch since he'd consigned his to the Shannon Pot — the gang left, the echoes remained.

And the Interrogator set out. Approaching the stone stairway, he, in turn, was hailed by what's-his-face.

—Mr Boss-Man, what's the difference between a door and a *dooor*? Are ye right, Boss-Man, right, wait for it. A door, ye see, is made of boards, and a *dooor* is made of *booords* — right, Boss-Man, right? Up to the top of the class, Packy, and kiss the swanky mistress.

Warbling responsively, the Interrogator negotiated doors-on-doors, registered, in goodness of time, Kelly the dancer and Orr the ring-master, and, contented, stood before Sweeney.

Heavy on the air, raddle of symbiosis.

The Interrogator commenced.

—Here's a simple question. Sometimes you're very complicated for such a simple man, Sweeney. Here's my simple question.

Are you, Sweeney, or are you not, a liar? Congenital, in fact, liar? And, to compound misdemeanour, a breeder prolific of congenital liars? You and yours, Sweeney . . . Related, closely, question: are you, Sweeney, or are you not a killer? Congenital, in fact, killer, and, to compound felony, a breeder prolific of congenital killers? You and yours, Sweeney . . . And, Sweeney, addendum intimately related question, when not thus occupied, when freed from your perfervid proclivities towards lying and breeding liars, killing and breeding killers, in, Sweeney, your teeming and congenital spare time, so to speak, isn't your large occupation and dunt of pleasure, Sweeney, the howl prolonged and the whinge unending, that music for which you and yours are so justly celebrated across the civilised globe and even unto remote crevices of barbarian zones, the howl and the whinge in the dark of the day and the loop of the night for the paps of the world you never — *never* — had the moral courage to put your lipless mouth to?

Prolonged silence. A fashion of applause, it seemed to Sweeney, and, in truth, not undeserved. Nevertheless. Staring, humble creature, the floor, Sweeney offered comment.

—Yer a big fella when yer out. Like an ass's tool.

The Interrogator spilled laughter, asked Sweeney where he'd picked up that morsel.

—The mother to a cattle-dealer. Several lifetimes back.

—Any more, any others?

—I smelt more than I ate, Sweeney shifted into his pure back-of-the-bog drawl, and I ate more than I could afford.

—Encore.

They played that string for a while. Coffee then from a flask in the visitor's pocket, the potion shared, desultory, weather-gab, and, entirely relaxed, they came to the bit.

—I hate Fridays, the Interrogator loosed the *introit*, something about Fridays. Think they remind me of my late father as he limped to the grave.

He rose, walked the cell, sound of limb, stopped of a sudden.

—Where'd you get the lift?

—Near Monaghan.

—How near?

—Hen's race.

—Nature of vehicle?

—Tanker.
—Carrying?
—Pig's blood.
—Pig's blood?
—Pig's blood for the fields.
—Nutrition, eh?
—Larrup of the red stuff.
—For the fair fields of Erin-o . . .
—And I saw it.
—Saw it, did you?
—Sweeney was there.
—Describe it.
—Downpour.
—A downpour?
—Downpour of pig's blood, the growthy red rain.
The Interrogator resumed the walk, stopped, poised.
—Where'd you bail out?
—I bailed out at Ardee.

  —Know what he said to me last night, Sweeney, the fella? We're coming home from a film, and — roundin' a corner — says he — *Holdin' your hand is like milkin' a cow* — God's truth, Sweeney, that's what he said, I nearly foaled. You ever in love, Sweeney?
  That could only be little Nurse Kangley.
  —You ever in love?
  Sweeney delivered himself to airy recollection.
  —Her kisses — it was like being gobbled by feathers.
  —Are ye tellin' me? Kangley's eyes merrily intransigent, and then what happened if it's not an impudent question?
  Sometimes she reminded Sweeney of a fire-hydrant.
  —I almost wrote her once, he persisted, to wit and to woo — *A stóirín, I kept walking till I saw my head lyin' on the ground. My God, I'm dead, my head said, and me body fell over.*
  —Of course, it was quite evident, Matron laid it down and hammered it in, that what the rump of males, I believe, call *the woman question* was in there somewhere. It was, need I say —
  —Look at me.
  —It was quite evident in his general tone which — a matter of fond record — had two registers only, the rancorous and

the vituperative.

—Look at me with the guts of your eyes.

—Sedated, he was just about manageable. And — undeterred — I've been in the trenches, after all, for many's a day, Matron's student-nurses giggled ambiguous appreciation, I probed suppressions, depressions, impressions, inspissations, early memories —

—Trees . . . Timber . . .

Sweeney, humped on his dunce's stool, lurched to the pliable.

—Leaves . . . Branches . . .

—Keep it going, Matron switched gear on the instant, that's it, that's it, nurture a flow . . . .

—I'm three or four, Sweeney transformed to short pants and a sailor blouse, sunlit sepia, I'm racing among trees — away from the adults, mum, dad, summer afternoon, I'm being pursued down a rushy slope by Marie McNamee, there's uproar to frecken the crows, she's a neighbour, fiftyish, unmarried teacher, and she wants to be my bride . . . I ended up in the sheugh, *clábar* to the elbows.

He opened his eyes. The students had congealed to a fat knot, intense aubergine for whatever reason. Matron had an arm around him, honey-soap smell, and the frank whiff of a uniform freshly laundered.

—Keep it going, keep it going, nurture a flow . . . .

—An ash tree, there was no going back — really, he felt as if he were watching his bones fly past, in good order, an ash tree, huge on the lawn, loved by the child that was and the man who would be. In the dream I'm looking at a cleft in the butt of the ash tree . . . .

—Keep it going . . . .

—A scallop shell at rest there, as if thrown up by some freak tide of this far inland shore — or better, slipped out of the tree in the silence of days . . . I watched, rooted. The shell slowly begins to open . . . A chink, a breathing chink . . . Opens slowly the piecesheen further . . . Now — there it is, glimpse of pink, flesh-bud, pink-pulsing within. Owned me, all my seasons . . .

—We're watched, y'know.

—First time I ever talked to a woman through a keyhole.

—Never did anything else — if you had the wit to know it.

She allowed him into the hall, barred the road to the kitchen.

Very well. Fight it out right there.
  —What's stuck in your craw?
  That toughened her mouth.
  —Guess, Mister.
  —Cough it up, will you?
  —I want none of you here.
  —Busy with the busy bee?
  —Don't come by this place again.
  —All the juice he can suck.
  —Watch your lip.
  —'We talk mostly of you' —
  —Leave now, will you?
  They paused, shaken, equally, by the eruption. Looked at each other across the narrow of the hall, gave nothing. Went to it again, Sweeney in the van.
  —No calibrated last words?
  She searched, not for long.
  —We're ashamed —
  —'Ashamed'?
  Come, subfusc, come, taint us now and forever.
  —Yes, ashamed.
  —Glory be, 'ashamed' . . .
  —That's right, we're ashamed.
  —And for why 'ashamed'?
  —We're ashamed that you should be seen as you are —
  —As I am?
  —As you are, yes —
  —Yes, come on, 'ashamed', spill it, spill it —
  —We're ashamed that you should be seen as you are by those who knew you as you were.
  —So who do you love then, you shut of the lot?
  The kindness of strangers. She proffered salted peanuts.
  —Potato-bread.
  —Real son of the soil.
  She flashed grey-green eyes, verve of the estuarine.
  —Arguments.
  —In the jaw, all right.
  —Shine of a tom-cat, he gambled his lyric note, glidin' into long grass of August.
  —Human-kind?

—Don't press me.
—Human-kind?
Late-night bar. Once more an aubergine world. Was he turning to an egg-plant? A bruise? The juke-box sang — *With me ing-twing of an ing-twing of an eye-doo / With me ing-twing of an ing-twing of an eye-day / With me ooralem-rooralem randy / And me lovestone keeps bitin' away, away / Me love-stone keeps bitin' away*...
—There's one, he relented.
—I'm listening.
—Love my daughter.
With me ooralem-rooralem randy / And me love-stone keeps bitin' away...
—Yes, love my daughter.
She spoke to him through shadows of the mirror.
—Heart's needle, Sweeney...
—I know, I know...
Into shadows of the mirror they sang it together.
—Heart's needle is an only daughter.

The wood noised animal, vegetable, mineral, clear benediction but don't mitigate the undertow crackle, no theme-park this of the summer Sunday, salute industry of those sturdy tracker-dogs, applaud shimmy of the stoat, shrike's crimson badge against the green.
—Are you for the wood, Mr Sweeney?
Matling came in, from some pungent crevice of encounter.
—So I believe.
—Is the wood for you, would you say?
—I believe so.
Their radio meeting, wasn't it? The switchboards jammed. Disembowelling the enthusiastic vote. *Largo, per favore.*
A clatter of pigeons broke cover. He'd have sworn pigeons. When he looked twice, they were crows, the grey ones, shitting in unison — that for his benefit? — and flash of a knife, he noted, entering the wind's hello.
—Wicked, wicked the night, chilly the dart of morning, he reported to the met office — and threw in a defiant shout, we never died a winter yet nor bought the snow for crubeens.
Lost his balance, and fell through a world of branches, beech,

wings taking the brunt, found the limb of safety, steadied. Below, a mink took off, pong of the river, sigh in the bushes, gone.

—Still in it, Sweeney?

The madman. Sudden as soot, floating from an upper storey.

—A piece of me, Old Cock.

You've had a bad night, Sweeney registered. That right eye, button hanging from the winsome thread. Yet a purged swathe across the forehead.

—Sweeney?
—Yes, Old Cock.
—Our bodies a feast for birds of prey.
—Ravens our heavy silence.

They went to it, as well sing grief as cry it.

—Bent the nails.
—Worn the loins.
—Raw the thighs.
—The house gapes.
—That's the ticket.
—A comfortless nest.
—Heart of storm your only shelter.

And paused, greatly cheered. The madman offered watercress. The pair breakfasted, simple pleasures of the road, wood-road, sky-road, warrens waiting. Swinging from a stout branch, drinking watery sunlight, the madman wondered.

—Anybody know why sap rises?
—Ask the trees.

Savant Sweeney rattled his feathers — succulently, was inclined to primp, controlled himself.

—Juice of the watercress? the madman came again.
—Enquire the water, Mister Misfortune.
—*Pluck she grows . . .*
—*Pluck more, grows the more . . .*
—Time for a spin?

Sweeney spoke against the east wind, raged even. The madman spoke of thermals, assuasive. Sweeney doubted their existence — 'in this stretch'. Anywhere, really. The madman boasted familiarity. They took off, rousing every bird next or near, stretched their wings, relished whip of the wind.

—Our hinterland, Old Cock, Sweeney looked down possessively on the lakes and hills, bladder swelling near the eye.

—Do we frighten birds, Sweeney?

Sweeney glanced at his companion, solicitous, not that solicitous.

—No, they just shiver when they see us, Old Cock.

The east wind bit, and no sign of the promised thermals, not the colour. Far belling of the stags, chests expanding for the tippin' sayzon. They soldiered into the air-flow.

—See that valley to the south, Old Cock?

The madman took it in.

—Glenflesk, where they bate the childher for going hungry.

Sweeney primped now to the sting of reminiscence, and eased into his high *seanchaí* note. Nothing pleased him more than to weave the tale when cruising above the locale.

—I seem to remember — or am I making it up? — or is it making me up? — I seem to remember once in that valley. Night. Fog. The pure black-white juice. On a job. Three of us. Wire fence beside me. My hand drifts to the top wire. And I feel — it's in my finger yet — another hand on the wire. Few yards away, had to be. I steadied, let fly. Left four in ribbons. Once upon a time there was a warrior bold.

A moment's silence. The wind had toughened. What river was that below? Dromore? Fane? Sweeney remembered the Borora, tributary of childhood, let the sound fill his skull, lenitive, *Borora*, River of the Red Cow, Red Cow of the Full Moon, White Cow of the Young, Dun of the Dark.

—The other hand, the madman asked, through the wire, Sweeney?

—Yeh?

—What'd it taste like?

—A heart-beat.

The 'copter racket, as always, came from nowhere, the gunfire likewise. The two dropped like stones, endured bruises as they hit convenient timber with the brakes off, found cover, uttered prayers, settled, relaxed as the 'copter racket capriciously faded. They'd landed in a fine cedar.

—Beats any safe house I ever endured, Sweeney allowed.

Vertiginous cuntal smell of the wood. *Durate e servate*. Find the well where that juice pumps.

—Sweeney?

—Old Cock?

—Know what drove me to this?
—You told me.
—I've several versions.
Sweeney's story-teller's blood swung something understood.
—Let her rip.
—There was a battle.
—The forever battle.
—Dress for it, I argued.
—But of course.
—Don't go like tramps.
—Paddy Pig and Micky Muck.
—Wash.
—Perfume your limbs, Sweeney stretched, caressing the cedar caressing him.
—Vest your bodies for death.
—*La Grande Horizontale.*
—They turned on me, Sweeney.
—Bombs in their sleeves.
—Drove me to where you find me.

Ripple of thunder, and flourish of a storm nearing the wood. And, neither far nor near, summons of a rifle-shot. The cedar bustled. Exuberantly, the madman gloomed.
—What do you want on the stone, Sweeney?
—Let me think.
—If you have to think, it's useless.
Sweeney took the wallop, rose.
—*Survivors will be persecuted* . . . You?
—The marvels, the madman closed his eyes, *mean the marvels.*
—*Mean the marvels*, Sweeney balanced it.
—Came to me in a whisper, the madman opened his eyes, what to do about the marvels? *Mean them.*
Sweeney looked at him, loved him forever.
—Shure isn't that it?

Thunder again, close. And again. Praise we the Gods. The Mothers, while we're at it. Raindrops, lucent. From the very fount, the waters broke.

He heard the sound of nuts being cracked, and somehow he knew: a particular meeting, long pending, was imminent. Dropping quietly through the lime tree, he — directed by the sound — travelled a limb, looked down into the glade. It was she. He presumed it was she.

—I'd ate hazel nuts to a band playin', she squawked to the stone in her hand, admonished the nut under assault, come on, ye divil ye, don't be thick with me now.

He dropped into the glade.

—There y'are, Sweeney, she didn't even look up.

—You've atin' and drinkin' there.

—Join the picnic, she belted away at the nuts, I was waitin' for ye, childybawn. Are ye famished as ye look?

—Do with a bite, he forced etiquette, they'd be fighting soon enough.

—Or maybe two, she'd an answer for everything, sit down there, will ye, before ye take a stannin' wakeness.

Uncomfortably, he settled, keeping to her left side. Rapine was the note. Well, with the shield or on it.

—Try that handful, she gave him a portion of the readied nuts, they're how the salmon leps, I always heard.

He was surprised to hear himself utter sedate thanks. Then he had been well brought up, be the death of him some day. They munched. He wouldn't look her in the eye. Only the whites, he'd been told somewhere.

—Who are you? he watched a pismire promenade across the stone that was her hammer, if I might ask?

—To be sure ye might ask.

—What's that mean?

—Ye don't know me?

—Who are you?

Laughter from her now, it came from a bad place.

—I'm the one ye never met, Sweeney, ye never talked to me through no keyhole, busy as ye were on yer hunkers.

She took a fit of spluttering.

—Always a bad one in any fistful. You in yer health, Sweeney?

—Improving, I do believe.

He was watching it now.

—Ye tell me? she jeered, findin' yer health in the wood, are ye? From the look of ye, ye couldn't push a cat off a stool.

Again she cleared her throat, hawked a shower of spit past his right shoulder.

—Excuse the bad rearin', Sweeney. I do love to ventilate the thrapple at regular intervals. Yer very quiet.

She resumed the dedicated nut-cracking.

—Maybe yer wise, she crooned, there's far too many makes a knot with the tongue the teeth can't loosen. I'll be open with ye, Sweeney, ye've found yer place in the procession.

—Great.

—Ye knew the one before ye.

—Who was that?

That shallow breathing his?

—Yer old friend McDonagh, the croon with back-slap this time, I landed on his shoulders, Sweeney, light as the bumble. And ye remember the details . . . .

He said nothing: she free-wheeled on.

—One day firin' from the far nook he smashes the binoculars instead of borin' the skull, and — isn't life the divil? — it got into him, the wee mistake, it got at him, the poor clob, and from that second no more droppin' them like apples from the sunny side of the tree. His wits left him on account of a few bits of measured glass skitin' — when it could have been another skull quietly holed, and his double figures soarin'.

She flapped her duds.

—May he rest aisy. I'd weep if I'd the tears to spare.

Querulous whine of the wind, menacing patter from the leaves. Back to the nut-cracking.

—Will you for Christ's sake stop cracking those nuts.

The phoney war was over.

—Oooh . . . Now will ye listen to him?

—I'll take you on.

—Will ye so?

—You needn't bare the teeth.

—What need? she sprang to her pins, hooped over him, what need — when I have ye by the hasp of the arse? And for why? Ye never loved, ye *stumpán*. Because ye never loved yer lost in the wood, and yer lost in the wood because ye don't know the trees, and ye don't know the trees because —

—Try me, he rose to meet her.

—That I will, she lifted one leg and closed arms across her chest, oak?

—Oak for shelter.

—Ash?

—For fight, for fight.
—Hazel?
—Hazel for wand.
—Beech?
—For nest.
—Holly?
—Holly for door.
—Apple?
—'Do you love a pear?'
—Birch?
—For scar.
—Briar?
—Briar for blood.
—Aspen?
—A bundle o' nerves.
—Yew?
—For coffin, yew for coffin.
—Elm? Well? Elm? Elm?
—Elm for rot.

Bested, she took breath. Now he examined her: as reported, two off-white pools, far back in the head, lifeless, bar the suction — which was not trifling. He looked away.

—Jaysus, yer not as stupid as ye look, she rallied, I was always told they had to make up letters after z for ye in High Infants.

—Where's that fog coming from?

He could scarcely see his hand.

—From the air, Sweeney, that's where fog comes from. Yer not suggestin' it's comin' from my pleats and plaits, are ye?

She was no longer to be seen but a mélange of sinister hopping sounds announced the arrival of her vicars-general. He could see them soon enough. Five trunks, headless, the severings red circles that shone in the murk, and five heads of the trunks skipping beside them, and five more grizzle-heads without body or trunk.

—Parcel him in timber, the hag screeched, gut him.

Sweeney took off, cutting down an aisle convenient before sheltering in a great copper beech. But active sheltering. He was making for the roof of the tree, and the best of his play. Already they were underneath him, swarming the lower branches, baying destruction.

—Come back, ye cowardly whelp ye, he heard her behind them.

The yapping and the howling grew intimate. He saw blue above, steadied, braced for shameless take-off — and, remembering the primal prophylactic, changed his mind. As he turned into the furore, they were a mere two yards below, goat-head, dog-head, wolf-head, the seething ash-grey cluster stippled copper in the vat of the beech, howls scorching his pinions as he wrapped close, and the pulse thinned.

Look them in the eye . . . .

He did, he had, and — to see it work . . . Split-second stand-off, they hung there like an exhalation from the sinks of hell. *We'll be back*, was the whiff, noisome, from their beaks — those were beaks not mouths. Their eyes — they'd all the same eyes, an eldritch sienna brown — fermented malediction, even as they dimmed. The foliage crackled, shone unsullied. The tree unwound to farthest root.

Treasure the clouds, was his prayer for weeks after. He went for a spin. Low cloud gathered him, and, keeping to that cover, he coasted for hours, knew the healing. It was night by the time he left it. High in the southern sky, he saw Cygnus, Lyra, and Aquila — and would have hugged them. Some miles eastward the wood waited. Home.

—I found the heart's thermals, he told Old Cock the next day, and going the long way home I sang, over and over I sang what saved me — if I was to be saved. Oak for shelter, ash for fight, hazel for wand, beech for nest, holly for door . . .

—Apple, Old Cock touched his well-tempered clavier, do you love a pear?

—Birch for scar, briar for blood, aspen a bundle o' nerves . . .

—Yew, the madman embraced one, red she shoots, green she sings, yew for coffin.

—Elm? Sweeney in a low voice addressed all the wood, elm? Are you there, elm? Are you there? Are you there?

The two listened.

—Elm for rot, the wood replied.

The frost-bird flew. Time for it, had he not sought it, maybe even earned it, suffered it into — being, no, don't go that far, the Greeks had a word for it, and swift the blow. Be content with the frost-bird flew, one and one makes three, taken the long day. The frost-bird. Armed. Esurient. Vengeful. Aware — in possession of all the files — of the precise thickness and extent of carapace for stripping. And would not be denied.

—Water's the strongest thing in the world, Die Brocken one night intoned, steam's the second, the third is wind.

—What about the cold? a woman high in the waist and a drop to her mouth put in, what prize — would you say — for the cold?

Certo. Well, they'd signed for that blast, their eyes flickered that, behold — at a glance, measure it in points of our blue eyes, allow that it wavered, looped to transparence, went under, allow it returned — like the truth, or a wraith of the truth, variable knowledge of glove-off-the-paw, let that chill bite, and thole, thole, thole my hearties.

They sat in the trees. Looked around, any morning. White iron the cut of the world, melt the eyes in your head, and cinder your third. Earth rang, water stared, breath swivelled, we gaped from the trees — and sang dumb, the white grip, yes, but more wickedly etched, no song in us, the long ago fork lost stolen or stray'd, so there for the note, the note, to learn the note. Or go deaf in the Lighthouse. Those odds.

The tremendous release of going for an answer: you wouldn't wish it on the neighbour's child. One answer. An answer for starters. The question that weighed, who owned it? This world all about, white world of come-if-you-dare, who'd possess it, who'd meet the load? Or ponder the larger: sweet spindrift globe, busy planets, callisthenics of stars, we were in it, and of it, somehow we *were* it but no gullet open to loose — *Who'd meet the load?*

Motherings of blindness. Listen hard to the (frozen) river. And you'll catch, they say, the fish. Can you see? It pertains. Yes, blindness, the worst, blindness of everything settled and known, known weather, known road, known plot of ground. So to sleep, wrapped in turf-smoke. The basket battalion. Glaucoma, cataracts, involuntary lobotomy and related mishaps.

And now, frost-bird flying, the fissures gleaming. Can you learn to shiver, you there on the slippery branch? Too late? Too early? Too long? Too short? One in ten, say, flourished, beneficent dereliction of the heart's needle, bright as Aldebaran. You don't mistake that eye. Fair percentage, the times were in it, support-system, fragile but there. Lesion of thresholding insight — rush of blood, the left hemisphere. Perception's rubric.

Maybe salvation's.
 To name, that be it? That must be it, their action necessitous. No question of jumping till driven but, crutches on fire, the jump to the deed. Naming. Hooped in bothawns of nothing we named, lips fumbling to it, named frost-fern and frost-itch, frost-dew and frost-bow and frost-smoke a weight on the pools. Gave tongue like the beagles of morning. It wasn't worth the steam of our piss.
 —A looking away, Old Cock diagnosed.
 —Our backs to the front.
 Die Brocken's simple tongue.
 They'd stayed strangers, named subject — and object — as strangers. The bland invitation. And roasted for that, oh hummed on the spit. It gathered, came at them, black frost and white, diamond and button, and wreathing the chain. They were stuck to the trees, they'd be one with the bark if this weather held. Jocund and climbing, the frost-bird wrote ampersands, shat on them from almighty heights.
 Bhí go maith. We ate of the rime, that was next on the card, looking up from the plate. Another out offered, to eat but not tasting. Lots bought it, shackled, afeared, buds drew back and shut shop, and who'd blame them? No sugar-fix this, vintner's emollient, bathroom placebo, this be earth's frozen mist. Eat. Taste. Swallow. Digest. Defecate. *Ça va?*
 Sweeney tasted, no knowing what sustained. The nerve ravelled. Dug in, he called for a talisman. It came. Cherish the ailment, *felix culpa* the name on your door. He drew on his scars, and invisible scars, from shingles and scabies to tinnitus of evening, anomie of dawn. And slipped past the sentries — in that guise. And tasted. What'd she taste of? She tasted the here and she tasted the other, flavour of Elsewhere, flavour of earth that stores its gone down.
 Every day seemed beginning. And end. We're talking time. And bones. Stung cheek-bones we humped there. I watched, I waited, I counted all colours of gone. I listened, I was learning that decade, Old Decade of the Listening Ears. Listening for word, and word wouldn't come. Come when I'm ready, said word, come when I'm spoken. And back to the bunker.
 We cursed blood.
 We fell empty.
 We dwindled to blades on the bough.

Morning struck morning. Let the cup pass — of course. Go home, mind the tongs from the fire — believe it. Waltz like the rest, enraged vegetable in trousers, why not? Temptation, the dulcet lisp of silk on silk, played him lavishly. Nod, all that was needed. Great reckoning — in a little room, two-third way up a sycamore. The silk-note. That also to be tasted.

—*Volens ducent, nolens trahunt,* Die Brocken roared each evening to the jandied sun.

A man the sum of all his actions. Never mind his contradictions.

What kept you going?
Badness.
Too far in to turn back.
Lure of the storm.
A daughter.
My good friends the branches.
Voice of the tides.
Islands, a memory, islands like cats on the warm morning rug of the sea.

The thaw arrived. It's a ruse, said Old Cock. No one listened. The sunlight was clamorous, thunder the quick sound of water. The afflicted shook themselves, began to talk in whispers. A blackbird screeched — they'd forgotten such choirs lived. We drank from the melting branches. One, in delirium, took a cold shower, grimacing under a fir tree while his companions tramped the limbs above. Any moment, the thaw would stream. Old Cock demurred.

As the light left, the frost-bird flew past, glider, tree-top height, like an omen of the merciless.

With night the hurricane came, drew back while frost fell like boulders, returned, went to it. Here was the meeting, if meeting to be. Nowhere to hide — the trees refused, that was their vein, they were right, it was over, nowhere to hide — unless in defeat.

Bow —

White hurricane stirred, white hurricane lifted, white hurricane blew, white hurricane roared and said *Give*, yield to the blaze, eat of this hour, dread it passing and not returning. *Nowhere to hide*, the word was out, and *For whom are you saving it?* the word was in. The hurricane sampled its roar, loved it, upped it, roar welding the two worlds, paternoster of undertow worlds

wheeling beyond those again.
   For whom are you saving it?
   In the end it was simple as taking a glass of milk. At some point of the night, when he'd had enough, he said — Well, I will so . . .
   And was free (sortov).
   And, as in all the books, a rush of percipience: how easy — now it's done, how easy! And, as in all the books, sweet bitter of beestings, that's yours for doing over and over. And over.
   Those dunts for later.
   Thus the woeful night of the bowing, not general, some bowed, most went under, some bowed, and come morning, ripe morning, coldest morning of all, those humbled ones roused to the known.
   Sing it, Sweeney —
   White scorched the white, marrow flamed, we took in the scorch, no more evasion, we named without looking away, we tasted — no tasting as strangers, buds this time *en fleur, en chaleur*, we bought it — private treaty and public and *caveat emptor*, rose up in our bothawns of nothing and claimed it, a knowing at last, our fire, our anvil, our shape that would be, our smoke from the rib, our fern in the glass.
   Frost-bird flew past, morning's delicate gamboge its candle to breast.
   —*Morituri te salutant*, Sweeney, ebullient, waved.
   The candle-flame flowed, swayed, flowed, firmed on a spendthrift rose doré. Frost-bird vanished above the trees.

Acknowledgements

The first five stories in this book were published first in *Dance the Dance* (Faber and Faber, 1970). Nine appeared in *The Harper's Turn* (Gallery Books, 1982). Acknowledgement is due to the editors of *Cyphers*, *Image*, *The Irish Times* and *Irish University Review* where uncollected stories were published first and to Radio Éireann where 'Wing-Beat, Wing-Feather' was broadcast.